THE CARROT AND THE STICK

by

C. P. VANNER

CHIMERA

The Carrot and the Stick first published in 2001 by
Chimera Publishing Ltd
PO Box 152
Waterlooville
Hants
PO8 9FS

Printed and bound in Great Britain by
Omnia Books Ltd, Glasgow.

THE CARROT AND THE STICK

C. P. Vanner

This novel is fiction – in real life practice safe sex

'Why do so many men like to spank a girl's bottom?' Beth asked.

The female psychiatrist had not expected the question but was ready with an answer.

'The female bottom is the most beautiful part of the human anatomy,' the psychiatrist said. 'It is the portal to paradise, to the hidden chambers of pleasure.'

'But why spank it?' Beth persisted.

'Power and dominance,' the psychiatrist said. 'The priapic male is the hunter, the submissive female the victim, the more submissive the better.'

'Oh,' Beth said, disappointment in her voice. 'Is that all it is?'

'No,' the psychiatrist said. 'That is not all. There is another hidden truth behind the obvious.'

Beth was puzzled. 'What can that be?'

'Come over here,' the psychiatrist said. 'And I will tell you. Lie over my lap and I will show you.'

Chapter One

'Do you remember our deal?' Richard Cross looked up sharply as he spoke. 'About the carrot and the stick?'

Beth stirred on the comfortable couch yards from his desk in the big office. She tried to look unconcerned but felt her stomach lurch.

'Vaguely,' she said. 'Is that why you wanted to see me?'

He snorted. 'Vaguely. You were quick enough to accept it when I waved the carrot under your nose at Christmas.'

Beth's fingers strayed to the top button of her blouse. How could she forget it? Some carrot; a diamond pendant in a gold setting on a long, heavy gold chain. She owned nothing more beautiful or valuable.

'More carats than carrots, you will vaguely recall.' Sarcasm dripped from his voice. 'Twenty-two carats in the chain and more than a handful in the diamond. That's quite a bunch of carats.'

Beth smiled, trying to ingratiate herself. 'Of course I remember, Richard. How could I ever forget? I was only teasing you.'

Richard Cross ignored her attempt to lighten the tone of the conversation. 'And do you remember why you got it?'

'Because my figures were up,' she said.

'And now?'

Beth could not meet his eyes. 'They're down,' she muttered, wishing she was somewhere else.

'Yes, they're down.' He leaned back in his chair, relaxed and at ease. 'After the carrot comes the stick. I want you to report to me here after the office closes at six-thirty.'

Beth spoke hesitantly. 'What do you mean by... by the stick?'

But Richard Cross had already picked up a folder and was studying it. 'Here,' he repeated without looking up. 'After six-thirty.'

Damn. Damn. Damn.

Beth sat at her desk staring out of the window. She was angry with herself, not with Richard Cross. How could she have been so stupid? The youngest and best account manager, and among the highest paid, in Cross, Carstairs and Denton and now she was in danger of blowing it all.

The sunny June afternoon outside her window taunted her. If only there was snow on the windowsill and it was last December all over again. The office Christmas party had been the best evening of her life. Richard Cross had made a speech naming her manager of the year. He smiled into her eyes as he opened the red velvet box containing the necklace, and looked down, still smiling, as the diamond pendant slid into the cleft between her breasts which were proud and firm and almost completely revealed by the low cut evening dress. Privately she thought the diamond belonged there, beauty complementing beauty. She felt his warmth and the slight caress of the back of his fingers as he fastened the catch behind her neck.

Richard Cross was more than her boss; he was her mentor. He was fiftyish, but looked younger and was the only partner still working. Henry Carstairs and Cautley Denton had seats on the board and appeared about only once a month.

A year ago, Richard called Beth into his office late one afternoon. Her nervousness soon evaporated. It had not seemed at all like the meeting of an office junior and the senior partner. He praised her work, told her that she had a future in the advertising business and said he was prepared to gamble on her. A senior account manager was leaving; Beth Forrester, still only in her early twenties, would be his replacement. Did she agree?

Did she agree? Beth was so overcome she could not find the voice to say yes. She nodded, aware of an inane smile on her lips. She heard hardly another word.

'In this business we judge success by results,' he had said. 'Half yearly results. You will be responsible for three accounts worth three quarters of a million pounds. Increase them, and that is success. If they decrease, that is failure. Do you understand?'

Beth was miles away. She saw herself in her new office, sitting behind her new desk in her new outfit. Not just one new outfit but lots of new outfits.

'Do you understand?' he said again.

Beth had nodded. She had no strength and no desire, it seemed, to do anything but nod. 'Yes, Richard,' she croaked. She used his first name shyly. Although it was office practice to use first names on all occasions, she had never said his to his face before.

His stern expression relaxed into a smile. 'Beth, you are a daydreamer, which is good in moderation, and I have noticed you can be an idler, which is bad at all times. This is your big chance, your big challenge.'

'You won't be sorry,' Beth had gabbled. 'I shall—'

He cut in before she could go on. 'I am going to make you a deal. We shall operate on the carrot and stick principle. If you do well you will be rewarded. If you do badly you will be…' he paused, '…you will be punished.'

Beth had stopped listening at the word rewarded. Rewarded. Her mind leapt off into a dozen flights of fancy. Bonuses. Holidays. Luxury hotels. Flights on Concorde.

'Is it a deal?'

His stern voice brought her back to the present. She nodded again, a lock of her thick blonde hair falling over one eye.

'Yes,' she had said eagerly. 'It's a deal.'

As she left, Richard Cross laughed out loud. 'I don't think you've heard a word I've said in the last ten minutes.'

It had been a laugh full of amusement and anticipation.

Now, locked in the executive ladies' loo as the office emptied out for the evening, that conversation of a year ago echoed in Beth's ears. But now all she heard was the word she had ignored at the time: *punishment*.

She looked in the mirror as she reapplied her make-up with unusual care and precision. But why? Was she going on a date or to meet Madame Guillotine? The butterflies in her stomach flapped their wings more violently now than they had done all afternoon.

She was glad she was wearing her smart grey suit and peach blouse. At the same time she wished she could go home and change. She wished she could go home and stay there.

As she dabbed scent behind her ears and in the V-neck of her blouse, she straightened her shoulders. Richard was right; she had let the company down. Just a month ago Tyland Brothers cancelled its account, worth a cool half a million a year. In one cold and casual moment, Cyril Tyland had cost her and her company more than double the extra business she brought in during the autumn, the extra business for which she had been so well rewarded at Christmas. If only she could go back one month, just four weeks.

'Bloody man,' she said to the mirror. 'Silly me. Silly, silly me,' she added.

She looked at her watch and was horrified to see it was almost six-fifty. She felt a knot of anxiety in her stomach as she headed hurriedly for the door.

'If you care to submit your resignation, I shall accept it.'

At his words, Beth felt as if she had been punched in the stomach. Her knees were weak and she desperately needed to sit down, but Richard had not invited her to. She leant her fingers on a table covered with business magazines.

'But...' she gasped. 'But I don't want to resign.'

He looked grim. 'You should have thought of that before you started losing business. I warned you that this is a rough trade. There is no place for losers.'

Beth shifted her feet but judged that this was not the right time to ask to sit down.

Richard studied her, leaning back in his comfortable chair and toying with an ornate letter opener. She thought how very attractive he was even when he was stern and unbending. Especially when he was stern and unbending.

'What on earth has happened to you?' he said, and she thought a little of the ice in his voice had melted. 'You're not the girl you were. You are not with it any more.'

She hung her head and shifted her feet again.

'So you don't want to resign?'

'No,' she said, truly appalled at the thought. 'No, I don't. I really don't. Please give me another chance.

'Please may I sit down?' she added, after a brief but

tense silence.

'No,' he said. The ice had not melted. He sat thinking for a moment or two.

'You're dealing with the Rybix people, aren't you?' She nodded but he was already going on. 'Let that be your last chance; bring in that account, or else.'

At his words she exhaled the breath she felt she'd been holding since entering the office. 'Thank you, Richard.' She had to hold herself back from running to him and kissing his hand. 'Thank you, I won't let you down. You won't be sorry.'

She turned to go and he let her get almost to the door before he spoke. 'Where are you going?'

She froze in her tracks. 'I thought… I thought we had finished.'

He shook his head slowly and deliberately. 'The figures,' he said. 'The last half's figures. You lost this company almost half a million pounds.'

'I'll make it up.' She was holding her breath again.

'You need something to wake you up,' he went on, ignoring her. 'Now let's see. You brought in extra business worth two hundred thousand and you received a necklace worth seventeen and a half thousand. You lose business worth almost half a million so…' he appeared lost in thought, '…so what do I do?'

She hardly heard the question; she was marvelling at the cost of the necklace. She had no idea.

'So what do I do?' he repeated sternly.

'I don't know,' she replied meekly.

'Carrots and sticks,' he said. 'Rewards and… and what?'

She looked lost so he repeated it. 'Rewards and what?'

'Punishment,' she whispered.

'Yes, punishment.'

'So what is this stick you are going to beat me with?' Beth asked, cringing because her nervousness made her words sound cheeky. 'A financial penalty? Extra work?'

Richard looked up sharply. 'You think I'm joking?'

'You're not?'

In reply, he nodded towards a carved drinks sideboard against one wall. In former, more pleasant times she would have already been invited to fetch the vermouth bottle and two glasses from one of its cupboards.

'You'll find what you are looking for over there,' he said.

Beth was startled and flustered. Did he want her to get him a drink? On unsteady legs she approached the sideboard and noticed immediately the only thing on its polished surface. How had she not noticed it before? It was as thin and as sinister as a snake basking in the evening sun. A cane. A bamboo cane about four feet long, the dull yellow of the bamboo standing out clearly against the polished redwood. She picked it up as if it would bite and looked at him questioningly.

'Carrots and sticks,' he said.

'You can't… you can't mean…' Her voice was little more than a croak. She tried to sound flippant, to lighten the atmosphere. 'What am I supposed to do, hold out my hand or something?'

He smiled faintly. 'Or something, I think,' he said. 'Not your hand but some other part of your anatomy.'

'You mean…' She was again unable to bend her tongue around the words. 'You mean… my bottom?'

'It is customary, I believe.' He nodded to himself. 'Especially for naughty girls.' She stared at him mutely, so he continued, without smiling. 'If you care to submit

11

your resignation, I shall accept it.'

'But I don't want to resign,' she expostulated without thinking and then, a second later, realised what she had said. She had made up her mind without thinking. She would rather be caned than lose her job. She found she was still holding the cruel implement of punishment in her hands – and without another word she offered it to him.

As she did so something extraordinary happened inside her. Her body became disconnected from her brain. In her mind she felt only dread, even fear, but her body interpreted the situation differently. Waves of warmth began to ripple outwards from her groin, suffusing her from top to toe. Like waves hitting a rock on the shore, the ripples doubled back on themselves until she felt almost giddy. Her knees were even weaker than before and she thought she might fall. She realised with shame, amazement and an intense thrill that she was very sexually aroused.

So powerful were the emotions she imagined they must show and that Richard would read her mind. She pressed her thighs firmly together under her skirt. There was nothing she could do about the blush on her cheeks or the unusual brightness of her eyes. She wished she had time to fathom out what had happened to her. It was almost as if, by offering Richard the cane, she had unlocked a hidden passion. And with this thought came a sense of *déjà vu*, that it had happened this way before and that it was right.

Richard was studying her closely. 'Do I gather you accept your punishment?'

Beth held her head up. 'Yes,' she said. 'So long as it is administered by you.'

He nodded. 'It won't be easy for you,' he said. 'And it

won't be over quickly. Somehow I have to work out a punishment worth double the value of the necklace. That's a lot of punishment.' He paused and then sat forward. 'So here is what I propose; I punish you as often as I want, in any way I want, and at any time I want for a month. A month today it will be over. You will have paid your penalty. Is that reasonable?'

'Yes, I suppose it is,' Beth said quietly. 'And when would you like start?'

'I can see no point in putting it off,' he said, and she held her breath again. 'Check and make sure the office is empty and then return here. I shall cane you as if I was the headmaster of a girls' school and you have been sent to me because of some breaking of the rules.'

'Yes, sir,' she said, somewhat taken aback by this last statement.

But Beth was glad to use her legs again and to have a moment to herself. She flitted around the office trying to calm herself and to work out what was happening. He was actually going to cane her on her bottom. Her bottom. Would he expect her to be naked? How many strokes would he give her? Could she take it? Would he make sexual advances as well? And if he did, what would she do?

Her thoughts tumbled over themselves, questions but no answers. The excitement was overwhelming; she dreaded the ordeal, the expected pain and the humiliation, but at the same time she wanted to submit to the man. She wanted him to chastise her, to use her, to debase her. It was as if she was taking part in a film, a pornographic film that had reeled through her mind at night when she took the solace of a lonely single girl lying in bed with her hand between her thighs. He had mastered her then; he was to master her now.

Richard stood with the cane in his hands when she returned without knocking to his office. She stood demurely in the middle of the floor, her feet together and her hands clasped in front of her. 'I have come to be punished, sir,' she said.

He sat on the edge of his desk. 'Remove your skirt and top,' he commanded.

Slowly and carefully she undid her jacket and skirt, slipping them off and placing them neatly on a chair against the wall.

'And the blouse,' he said.

With unsteady fingers she unbuttoned the blouse and placed it on the suit before resuming her position. She knew well the figure she presented; she had admired it often enough in the mirror in her bedroom.

Despite her trepidation, Beth felt proud as he looked her over deliberately, from head to toe. He took his time absorbing her innocent beauty. She knew well what he could see; high heels the colour of apricots, long, bare, brown legs, skimpy peach-coloured knickers through which a faint shadow of pubic hair could just be seen. A flat and deliciously toned stomach that led up to the matching peach bra, which encased and displayed her magnificent breasts; breasts – she had been told – as enticing to lick and gorge on as ice creams on a sweltering day. Above them her slender throat and impish face, made to smile but unsmiling now, and her soft fair hair.

'Turn around,' he said. She did as she was told, standing straight, knowing he would be looking at her bottom and knowing too that he should like what he saw. It was firm and round, the cleft between the cheeks emphasised by the hug of her knickers. Any moment now, she thought.

Any moment now he'd tell her to take her knickers off.

She heard the swish of the cane. He was swinging it as he approached her. He stopped in front of her and placing his free hand under her chin, tipped up her face to look her in the eyes. She felt again the warm ripples flowing outwards from her sex and a dampness between her legs.

'Beth,' he said, 'I am going to give you six strokes of the cane. Bend over and touch your toes.'

She was momentarily crestfallen; he did not want to see her naked. Slowly she bent in front of him, parting her legs slightly so she could better touch the floor. It was not particularly comfortable but she was a supple girl and it was a position she adopted many times at the gym where she worked out.

She could sense him inspecting her afresh, looking at the part of her anatomy most exposed and nearest to him. The knickers that covered her bottom were stretched and hid very little. She felt his hand at the waistband. Now, she thought. But instead of pulling them down, he tucked them up so that they resembled a g-string; a line around her waist, another line at right angles disappearing into the cleft of her bottom, and between her legs, a small pouch containing the lips of her sex.

He did not touch the unblemished flesh of her exposed bottom any more than he had to, and she was disappointed.

She heard his voice from behind. 'You deserve to be severely punished, Beth. This is going to hurt. It is for your edification. And,' he added quietly under his breath, 'for my pleasure.'

Hearing his words, Beth, with her head just a few feet above the floor, looked back at him between her own knees. She could see the front of his trousers, and with a sense of triumph she saw what she was looking for, the unmistakeable shape and presence of his manhood pressing the cloth outwards, seeming to seek her near-nakedness.

There was no more warning than that between the crack of a rifle and the impact of the bullet. She was just aware of the swish of the cane at the moment it cut into her tensed bottom. She cried out in surprise and then drew her breath in with a gasp as the pain hit her. She did not try to rise, but grasped her ankles with perspiring hands and let the pain wash over her.

'That's one, sir,' she said in a muffled voice.

Richard was in no hurry. She had just begun to relax and to unclench her bottom muscles when the second stroke landed, a fraction beneath the first. She cried out in pain this time and had to fight an overpowering desire to stand up and rub her poor flesh.

'T-two, sir,' she gasped, and instinctively opened her legs a little wider to steady her stance. This time there was no waiting. The third stroke landed on the softest flesh just above her thighs and she felt as though she had been cut in two with a sword. She bit her lower lip hard to suppress the howl that threatened to burst from her lungs.

'Th-three, sir,' she managed. 'I – I have been very naughty, sir, I know. But I'll be good—!'

The fourth stroke landed on the word 'good', and she ended with a yelp. It did not seem quite as hard as the others, or her bottom was becoming numb. She stole a look back at Richard again and the mound on his trouser front was even more prominent than before.

'Four, sir,' she said, when she could trust her voice to be steady.

'Yes,' she heard him behind her, 'you have been a

naughty girl… a very naughty girl.'

He swung the cane again and the fifth stroke landed in exactly the same place as the fourth, with renewed vigour. This time Beth sobbed and started to straighten up slightly, but with a strong hand he held her in position.

'F-five, sir,' she blurted obediently.

The sixth stroke landed with a crack that could have been heard down the hall, hard and with deadly accuracy across the fleshiest curves. Beth leapt up as if she was on a spring. She stood in front of him, tears in her eyes, lower lip trembling and her fingers gently cosseting the tortured flesh, marvelling at the ridges where only minutes ago there had been silky smoothness.

'Six, sir,' she panted when she had regained sufficient composure. 'Thank you, sir.'

She stood submissively before him awaiting his instructions, sensing that was what he wanted. He leaned back again against his desk with a faint flush to his cheeks, feasting his eyes on her delicious body.

Beth was proud of her stoicism and strength in the face of the ordeal. She was also acutely aware, now that the worst of the pain was subsiding, that the urgent warmth in her loins had replaced it.

'You can get dressed again,' Richard said, returning to his chair. The bastard, she thought as she picked up her blouse. He was playing with her. As she dressed she turned her back to him so he could see the welts on her bottom. Slowly and deliberately she lowered her knickers so that she was fully exposed before drawing them up again into their proper place.

'I can see that you are prepared to learn and to improve,' he said, when she was fully dressed. 'Tomorrow you have the Rybix people. Show me how much you have learned. Report to me here tomorrow evening at the same time.'

Standing by the door, Beth turned. 'Yes, Richard, and thank you for giving me a second chance.'

He had already bent his head to the papers on his desk. 'Rest assured, your lessons are not over yet,' he said.

Chapter Two

Beth stood in the carriage on the tube even though there were one or two seats available. She was too sore to sit. Anyone looking at her, and several men did, would have had no idea from her face of the thoughts cascading through her mind.

She surreptitiously smoothed her skirt over her buttocks, feeling again the welts under the cloth. If that is what it takes, my girl, that is what it takes. If you want to get ahead in business, if you want to do well, then you must take the rough with the smooth, the licks with the kicks. You deserved what you got, and you got it, with more still to come. Are you going to give in now? No, of course you're not. What really matters, a successful career or a sore bottom? No contest. And anyway, you took it well. Well done, you didn't cry, not much, and you didn't wet your panties. So he does it again, and again. So what? So what if it is humiliating to be caned on your bare bottom by your boss? If it works, it works. And it is going to work, isn't it? You are going to get the Rybix contract, aren't you? Richard can do all the punishing he wants, you'll show him.

As she approached her stop, Beth was proud of her resolve. Why then, did she feel so damned irritable? Sore and irritable. She realised with chagrin that it was the irritability that comes from frustration – from an unsatisfied sexual appetite.

She was in no mood therefore for petulance from Celeste

when she opened the front door of her flat.

Celeste was sitting on a sofa with her feet on the coffee table. 'You've ruined it,' she announced coldly.

'Ruined what?' Beth asked.

'The supper. I'd cooked a nice supper for us. You are always home by seven.'

Beth threw her leather briefcase into a corner with more force than necessary. She stood looking at the pouting nineteen-year-old. 'I'll come home when it suits me,' she pointed out. 'You are not my wife, you know. You are my flatmate. On sufferance,' she added, and then changed her tone. 'I've had a difficult day,' she said.

Celeste was not to be mollified. She stuck out her lower lip and theatrically picked up the evening newspaper and scanned it, holding it in front of her face.

'I'm going to have a soak,' Beth announced to the sports pages, before going through to the tiny bathroom.

She undressed as she ran steaming water into the bath, scented it, and thought that Celeste was just the sort of girl who would benefit from the treatment she'd so recently received. If ever a girl needed caning on her bare bottom it was Celeste. She was a pretty girl, and bright enough, but she was just plain lazy. Beth thought to herself how she would be glad to administer it herself, and given a little more provocation she might do just that.

Celeste had come to live with her two months before. Beth was originally from Newcastle and Celeste from Sunderland. Their parents were friends; both fathers worked for the same company and were golfing partners. The girls knew each other quite well but had never been real friends or playmates, mainly because of the few years' difference in their ages.

Celeste had left school the previous September and

devastated her parents by announcing that she had no intention of going to university. She wanted to go to London, she said, to be a model. Defeated, her indulgent mother wrote to Beth asking if Celeste could stay with her *until she finds her feet in London*. Beth could tell by the wording of the letter that Celeste's mother thought the capital to be a sink of iniquity just waiting to devour young female flesh. *Would you keep an eye on Celeste and keep her on a short rein*, Mrs Englund had written.

In theory and in practice Beth was actually quite glad of the company, and she would also have been glad of the rent money if Celeste just once came up with the full amount. But the girl did nothing. In her first ten days in London she had some second rate photographs taken of herself and made an amateurish composite portfolio, but since then she had seen no agents nor sought any interviews. Beth had no idea of how she spent her days but assumed they involved no effort of activity or industry.

What both flattered and disturbed Beth most was that Celeste seemed to live her life vicariously through Beth. She fed on all the details of Beth's working existence, her ups and downs, successes and failures. Most evenings Beth would have to give her details of her day, the comical moments and stories, often embellished, of office shenanigans. Celeste knew the names of all the people she worked with most closely.

It was not natural, Beth thought, picking up the lilac bar of soap. She should get a life. What Celeste needed, Beth thought again, was the smack of firm discipline. It would not have occurred to her before – before Richard had dealt with her – but that was just what Celeste needed, to have her knickers taken down and her bare bottom spanked.

With that thought, Beth turned over in the relaxing water and lay on her front. She closed her eyes, resting her chin on her forearm on the rim of the bath, and sighed with pleasure… and she was still like that when Celeste appeared. They would never lock the door on each other and would often have discussions, one in the bath and the other peeing or using the make-up mirror.

'I'm just reheating the…' Celeste paused in mid-sentence, transfixed by the sight of Beth in the bath, '…chicken casserole… What on earth happened to you?' Apart from her head and shoulders the only part of Beth to show above the bubbles on the water's surface were her buttocks, twin islands in a foamy sea divided by a ribbon of water. Instead of their normal unblemished beauty, they were ridged with red and purple weals.

Celeste fell to her knees beside the bath and reached out a hand, wanting but hesitating to touch them. 'What happened?' she asked again.

Beth rested her head on her arm and looked back down the length of her body. She could not quite see the focal points of Celeste's attention.

'Get the mirror,' she said, 'and show me.' Celeste lifted the mirror off the shelf and held it above Beth, adjusting it until she found the right position.

Beth studied her magnified bottom with awe and no small measure of pride. She had taken *that* and hardly cried out or shed a tear.

'You've been hit with a stick,' Celeste deduced, horror in her voice. 'Who did it?'

'Richard Cross,' Beth said, her voice muffled by her arm. 'But I deserved it.'

'Wow,' Celeste gasped. She had heard quite a lot about Richard Cross in their evening chats. 'Did he enjoy it?'

'Oh yes,' Beth chuckled, 'he enjoyed it. I could see that all right.'

Celeste ran her fingers gingerly over the ridges. 'I bet you didn't though, you poor thing,' she said. 'You are so beautiful, and he's so cruel.'

'It was that or the sack,' Beth said simply. 'I have cost the company a lot of money.'

Celeste picked up a large bath towel from the warming rail and held it invitingly. 'I want to hear all about it – every detail,' she said. 'But first let me make a fuss of you. You need something on it.'

Beth happily acceded. She felt like being pampered and the good-for-nothing Celeste might as well be good-for-something. As she stood up in the bath, Celeste enveloped her in the soft towel and began to pat her dry. The younger girl was as gentle as a mother with her baby, and when she put her arms around Beth to reach her back, their cheeks touched and Beth could feel her breath on her ear. Then taking down a smaller towel, Celeste sat on the floor and dried each of Beth's feet.

'I'll finish you off in the bedroom,' she said, putting her arm around Beth's shoulders and leading her out along the hall to Beth's bedroom. Gently pushing her shoulders she made Beth lie down, still wrapped in the bath towel, on the bed.

The evening sun flooded the room with a strong, warm light. Tenderly Celeste opened the towel as if she was unwrapping a present while Beth watched her handmaiden with grave eyes. She lay still, face up, her naked body gleaming like a pearl in a pink shell.

Celeste took the second towel and began to pat Beth dry, starting with her shoulders and then circling around and around Beth's breasts, which were firm and held their shape even though she was supine. Celeste took her time, teasing the small pink nipples with the towelling, and continued long after every drop of water had disappeared.

'That tickles,' Beth giggled.

Celeste towelled the flat stomach and the small patch of fair pubic hair which, when dry, was as soft and fluffy as a kitten's fur. Beth moaned and instinctively opened her legs slightly so that Celeste could dry the creases at the top of her thighs on either side of her labia. Slowly and gently, Celeste then rubbed the towel up and down the pink, inviting lips.

'What are you doing?' Beth asked, but there was no anger in her voice.

'Nothing much,' Celeste said huskily. 'Don't say stop.'

Beth placed an arm across her eyes. 'I'm not going to.'

'Tell me what happened,' Celeste said, her voice almost sounding too urgent in the quiet, sunlit room.

Beth spoke almost dreamily as Celeste continued the slow up-and-down movement against her sex. 'Richard caned me because of my figures – I received six of the best,' she said throatily. 'I deserved it. I accepted that necklace when I did well. I got this because I did badly.'

'Were you naked?' Celeste asked breathlessly. 'Turn over…'

Beth obeyed reluctantly; she had wanted that to go on forever. 'No,' she said, rolling gracefully over onto her stomach. 'In my undies. He pulled my panties up so they were like a g-string.'

Beth's back was already dry from lying on the towel, so Celeste patted it and her thighs quickly and then concentrated on her tender bottom.

'Did Richard do anything?' she asked, a tinge of jealousy in her voice. Very tentatively she placed her towelled hand on the punished flesh.

Beth winced. 'No,' she said, her head again buried in her arms. 'But I wanted him to.'

'Open your legs,' Celeste said. She dried between Beth's buttocks and again between her legs. She lowered her head and began to kiss the stripes on the warm flesh, counting aloud with each kiss. Beth did not move but drew her breath in with an audible gasp when Celeste kissed 'Five' where it crossed with 'Six'. Totally engrossed in her task, Celeste intuitively ran her tongue along the welt on the left cheek, down into the unmarked valley to Beth's pink and puckered anus, and then back up the other side, along the welt on the right cheek. Beth moaned with discomfort and pleasure.

'Don't move,' Celeste said, and disappeared off into the bathroom as Beth lay immobile in the evening sun. She was beginning to feel drowsy but was awoken when a blob of cold cream landed on one buttock. Celeste smoothed it in and then did the same to the other cheek.

'Richard taught me one thing,' Beth said.

'What's that?' Celeste asked, absorbed in her work, rubbing her hand in a circle around Beth's bottom.

'What I am going to do to you one of these days, if you don't pull your finger out.'

'Like this, you mean?' Celeste giggled, and she ran her greasy forefinger into the valley between Beth's cheeks and slipped it gently into the girl's anus. Beth groaned, as she cheekily eased it in and out.

'Yes,' she sighed, 'something like that.' She lay still, enjoying the delicious sensation. Celeste again put her finger into the cream jar and stroked Beth between her anus and vagina.

'A good spanking on your bare bottom might do you

the world of good,' Beth mumbled.

'Would it make me as hot as you are now?'

'We'll find out… very soon.'

'Promise,' said Celeste, and she slipped onto her knees at the end of the bed and put her face between Beth's thighs. Then she did with her tongue what she had done with the towel, licking up and down the length of Beth's labia. Beth, who had been simmering sexually since her encounter with Richard, relaxed and spread her legs wider to allow Celeste entry. Celeste's tongue penetrated Beth's moist and eager vagina while, with her right hand, she gently teased her anus. As the tongue darted in and out with increasing speed, Beth started to moan and to move her hips, but she still had time to think that the good-for-nothing girl was good-for-something after all. It may be unorthodox, it may even be wrong, but it was what she wanted, and wanted desperately at that moment.

As Celeste removed her tongue and ran it upwards along the line of perfumed ointment until it reached and tickled and teased her tiny anus, Beth could hear Richard's voice again announcing that he was going to give her six strokes of the cane. She lifted her bottom to Richard's cane, and to Celeste's tongue.

While Beth's bottom was still arched in the air, Celeste slid back down again and found the firm bud she sought and sucked on it as if it was a grape she wanted to swallow whole. Beth stopped thinking and simply felt. Her body knew it was finally going to have the release it had yearned for so long. She ground and rotated her wet sex against Celeste's mouth and tongue, moaning and grabbing handfuls of the duvet.

It was over all too soon. The movement of Celeste's firm moist tongue on her eager clitoris was more than

Beth could bear. Waves of liquid heat like molten lava surged and swirled through her loins until in one brief but timeless moment they exploded in a volcanic eruption throughout her straining body. Beth shrieked and clamped her thighs together on either side of Celeste's head, holding the younger girl still, her lips welded to Beth's vagina with an amalgam of cold cream and the intimate secretions of a female body at peace with itself at last.

The chicken casserole went cold for a second time as the two girls fell asleep together in the same bed.

Chapter Three

The Rybix building was in Victoria and Beth had time to get her hair done before her meeting at ten. As she strode through the glass and marble lobby at five to ten, she knew she looked good with her neat pageboy haircut shining above a white summer suit. Good enough to eat, she thought as she caught sight of her reflection in the darkened glass, and she blushed remembering the previous evening. She had never made love to a woman before; and she had certainly not thought of Celeste in that way. The girl had been sweet though, and suspiciously adept at what she did. But not so sweet and adept that she did not still need a damn good spanking.

Three men sat across the boardroom table awaiting her. 'The redoubtable Ms Forrester – alone,' said Jim Tyson, the Rybix marketing director, hardly bothering to stir from his seat to greet her. 'Travelling without your team this time?'

Beth sat. 'We're close to the end,' she said, laying her briefcase on the table. 'There should be nothing I cannot settle myself.'

'Perhaps Miss Forrester would like some coffee – I certainly would.' The speaker was a heavyset man in a Savile Row suit at the head of the table.

'Right away, T.J.,' Tyson said, and leapt up from the table and disappeared to talk to a secretary. Beth smiled her thanks to T. J. Kearns, the managing director of Rybix, and busied herself sorting out her papers on the tabletop.

T. J. Kearns was her man; the man who would make the final decision, the man she must win over to win the contract. Take it slowly girl, she told herself.

Nothing more was said until the coffee was poured. The third man, Charles Haigh, the finance director whose face was as grey as his suit, opened the proceedings.

'I'd like to start with the questions of debentures and default payments,' he said.

Beth patiently found the correct papers and started to negotiate. For half an hour she and Tyson and Haigh went over the contract details, ironing out differences and sorting out ambiguities and confusions. Kearns sipped his coffee and watched and listened.

When the conversation ground to a halt, he spoke. 'That seems quite straightforward,' he said to no one in particular. Then he fastened Beth with a piercing gaze. 'You are sticking to a three year contract at six hundred thousand per?'

'Yes,' she said, 'I would consider five but for a five year term.'

Kearns stood up and the others immediately followed suit. He offered his hand to Beth. 'We'll be in touch soon, almost certainly tomorrow.'

He held on to Beth's hand, pulling her gently through the door into the corridor. 'Come to my office when you finish up here,' he said quietly. 'Jim will show you where.'

Ten minutes later Beth stood in the lift and pressed the button for the top floor.

Once there, she found Kearns' secretary, Mrs Woods, who rose from her desk, a desk almost as big as Beth's office. 'How nice to see you again, Miss Forrester,' she said with a practiced smile. 'T.J. is waiting for you.'

She opened double doors opposite the lift and ushered

Beth inside. Across an acre of sumptuous carpeting, Kearns rose from his mahogany desk and approached his visitor. 'No interruptions, please,' he said to Mrs Woods, who was already quietly closing the doors.

He again formally offered his hand to Beth. 'The wunderkind of Cross, Carstairs and Denton,' he said flatteringly. 'Come and sit close to me. This place is so big it has drafts.'

He led her across the office to a comfortable easy chair, in front of and to one side of his desk. It gave Beth a chance to size him up properly. She was not fooled by his benign resemblance to Santa Claus in expensive tailoring. She knew he was a self-made man who could be and frequently was tough and ruthless.

'I hope I am not holding you up,' he said. 'I wanted a quiet word with you alone.'

'Not at all,' Beth said. 'I am at your service.' A voice inside her head was repeating like a mantra: be bold, face him like an equal. 'What can I do for you?' she asked.

'It is more a question of what I can do for you. Or rather, what I cannot do for you.'

Beth suddenly felt cold.

'You have been a very good negotiator,' Kearns went on. 'I think it is only fair to be honest with you now.'

For some reason Beth's confidence flowed away, and her voice became croaky. 'I don't think I want to hear this,' she said.

Kearns gave her a rueful smile. 'It was between you and AdWise. There's hardly anything between you but, on balance, AdWise offers the better deal. The official announcement will not be made until tomorrow but I thought, since you are here, I should tell you now in person.'

Beth was angry. 'So what have I been doing for the last hour and a half then?

'Don't be annoyed with me,' Kearns said mildly. 'This is business. I wanted to give you every chance. And you did well... very well.'

It was the kindness of his tone that did it. All the tensions of the last twenty-four hours seemed to catch up with her at once. She tried to stop herself, but tears began to flow and deep sobs shook her body. How pathetic, she scolded herself. How unprofessional... how *bloody* unprofessional. But still she cried.

Kearns seemed momentarily at a loss, and then he crossed the room and sat awkwardly on the arm of Beth's chair, putting one arm around her shoulders. She could smell talcum powder and an expensive aftershave lotion.

He patted her back. 'There, there,' he cooed, and her sobs slowly subsided.

Beth reached into her handbag for her make-up mirror as Kearns returned to his desk. 'God, I look a mess,' she said, looking into her compact.

'Not at all,' Kearns said. 'You are a beautiful girl. A very beautiful girl. And very clever too.'

'Not clever enough, it seems,' she said quietly.

'Not at all,' Kearns repeated with hearty jocularity. 'You're the future of the industry. The world, this world, is your oyster. It's only a small setback.'

Her tears welled again. 'No it's not,' she wailed. 'It's the end of the world.' How she hated herself at that moment. Not only had she not got the contract, but she was wailing like a baby in front of one of the most powerful men she knew. What on earth must he think?

Kearns suddenly seemed a little bored. 'It's not that bad,' he said dismissively.

She pulled herself together. 'It is, you know. It's my job. I lost one contract and I was punished. Just yesterday. Now I'm to lose this one. Two strikes and I'm out.'

Kearns' interest was rekindled. His eyes dropped to her knees and thighs as she rearranged her skirt and jacket, pulling herself together. 'Punished?' he said, almost tasting the word as he uttered it.

Beth nodded. 'This contract would have expunged my sins.'

'How were you punished?' Spots of colour had appeared on his cheeks.

'If you must know, I… I was caned, sir.'

'Caned? Where?'

'At the office.' She was not so distressed that she did not momentarily enjoy his discomfort.

'No, no,' he said. 'I mean, where were you caned?'

'Oh, on my bottom, sir.'

'Good heavens,' Kearns said, throwing himself back in his seat with an awkward laugh.

'On my bare bottom, sir,' she confirmed. 'Six strokes of the cane on my bare bottom.'

'I don't believe it.'

'It's true, sir,' Beth said. 'I can hardly sit down today. It's a good thing your chairs are well upholstered.'

'I don't believe it,' he said again.

'You would if you saw the marks,' Beth said without really thinking.

Kearns instinctively glanced at the door, then back at the lovely girl sitting before his desk. 'Show me then,' he said, a poker player calling her bluff. 'Mrs Woods won't disturb us.'

Beth shook her head. 'That wouldn't be right, sir.'

'I knew you were lying. What a drama queen, you are.'

But before he could say anything else Beth stood up, her jaw set. Without another word she removed her jacket and reached down and grasped the hem of her skirt. Slowly she raised it, revealing that she was wearing stockings and a suspender belt. The flesh of her thighs was creamy-white between the brown of her taut stocking tops and the pink of her panties.

Holding her skirt bunched in one hand, Beth demurely turned sideways to him as she hooked her other hand into her panties and eased them down. He had time for a glimpse of her pubic hair before she turned further and stood with her bottom exposed, her panties around her knees.

Neither of them said a word. Beth stood still, her bare bottom thrust out a little towards him. She glanced back over her shoulder. Kearns' eyes were fixed rigidly on her exposed flesh.

'Now perhaps you'll believe me,' she eventually said, her voice soft and gentle.

'That, um, that could be make-up,' he muttered. 'Come round here, a little closer.'

'Believe me, they're very real marks,' Beth said, her twisted panties stretched between her knees making her hobble a little around the desk. She stopped a few feet from him, turned away and lifted her skirt again.

Kearns leaned forward in his seat, his face on a level with her gorgeous bottom. 'Bend forward a little,' he instructed.

She obeyed, thrusting her warm globes towards him, and over her shoulder she could hear him clucking sympathetically as he surveyed the bruises.

'May I touch them?' he asked.

'Gently,' she replied.

He reached out and with warm fingers traced the breadth

of one of the welts. Beth felt them stop momentarily over the valley between her cheeks, and then she stepped away and dropped her skirt. Kearns sat back in his chair, visibly disappointed and panting slightly as she took her time adjusting her panties under her skirt.

'You must have been a very naughty girl,' he said as she resumed her seat. 'I won't ask you who did it; that is your business.'

She nodded. 'Let's just say I deserved it. I admit I can be a naughty girl – very naughty, at times. But that's all in the past now, with the contract going to AdWise.'

'Ah, the contract,' he said, seeming to have forgotten about it for a moment. 'Yes, the contract.' He was lost in thought for a while, then he pronounced, 'We don't formally make a decision or an announcement until tomorrow...' then his voice trailed off.

Beth said nothing. She did not want to interrupt his train of thought.

'AdWise is not a certainty,' he went on. 'There could always be a last minute change of mind...'

Beth remained silent. She was marvelling to herself over the effect her bottom seemed to have on men.

'Of course,' Kearns went on, 'if there was a last minute change of heart and the contract went to Cross, Carstairs and Denton, I would require your cooperation. Your *personal* cooperation,' he added, with plenty of meaning.

Beth nodded, breathlessly excited by the possibility of winning the contract after all. 'Naturally,' she said, 'that goes without saying.'

Kearns gave her a piercing look. 'That cooperation would have to be... how shall I put it... it would have to be intimate.'

'In what way intimate, sir?'

'Let me put it this way,' he said. 'The announcement is due to be made at three tomorrow afternoon. Suppose, just suppose, you were to come to me here at my office at twelve-thirty when Mrs Woods goes out to lunch.'

Beth held her breath.

'Suppose, just suppose, I was to ask you then to show me your bottom again, to see how the marks are.'

'Go on,' she whispered.

'And suppose, just suppose, I was to tell you then what a naughty girl you are and that I was going to take matters into my own hands.'

'I – I think I understand, sir, and I think that might be possible,' she said quietly.

'Then if that was the case,' the powerful man decreed, 'I imagine the announcement at three o'clock might well be different.'

'I am not sure that is ethical...' Beth said, '...if I understand you correctly.'

'Ethics, shmethics,' Kearns snorted. 'This is business. Ethics don't apply.'

'Are you sure?' Beth asked, a kaleidoscope of thoughts flashing through her mind – Richard's face, her office, a signed contract, a cane. She stood up. 'Well, I suppose I'll see you tomorrow then,' she said.

Kearns let her walk almost to the door before he spoke again. It was the old Kearns again, the man used to taking command. He called her by her first name for the first time. 'Beth, I would like to ask you a question. Take your time before answering. It's important.'

She turned and nodded. 'Of course.'

'If I asked you to show your bare bottom to a member of my staff – say, to my second in command – would you do it?'

Beth was nonplussed. She had not expected anything like this. She knew it was important, but it was not easy. If she acceded to the command and agreed to expose herself to someone else because Kearns wanted it, she would be demonstrating to him his authority and her submission. That, she guessed, might turn him on. On the other hand...

She quickly decided what the correct response should be. 'No T.J.,' she said. 'I wouldn't. My bare bottom and any discipline it might receive is strictly a subject between you and me. It is no one else's business.'

He nodded, apparently pleased by her answer. 'We'll resume discussions on that subject tomorrow,' he concluded.

'And discussions about the contract, of course,' she added, as she gave him an impish smile and reached for the door handle.

Beth was speaking into her mobile phone as she walked along the pavement. 'I think Rybix might be in the bag,' she declared.

'Think?' snapped Richard Cross. 'Might be?'

'We'll know tomorrow,' Beth said. 'I'm seeing Kearns at lunchtime.' The things she did for her career, she said to herself.

'And I'm seeing you this evening, don't forget, for part two of your lesson.'

'Yes, Richard,' said Beth, in her meekest tone. 'I haven't forgotten. I'll be in later. I'm going home to freshen up first. It's been quite a morning.'

Beth was still feeling pleased with herself when she opened the front door of her flat. She was, however, angered by what she found inside. The place was a mess. In the kitchen the congealed casserole was still on the stove, and the sitting room was strewn with cushions and fashion magazines. Beth stalked around the flat, her anger rising.

In her bedroom she found Celeste still asleep in her bed, on her front, the duvet thrown back and her slender legs exposed, her pouting sex peeping between her slightly parted thighs.

Beth slapped the nearest buttock hard, and a knot of unexpected excitement gripped her stomach as she watched the flesh quiver firmly. 'Y-you really are the limit, Celeste,' she stuttered, surprised by her unexpected reaction.

Celeste lifted her head, protesting and looking around in bewilderment at the same time. 'Wha... what are you doing here at this time?' she mumbled. 'Ow, that hurt,' she added, rubbing her bottom.

'Checking up on you,' Beth said shortly. 'And not liking what I find.'

Celeste rolled over and swung her feet off the bed. 'I've got to pee,' she announced sleepily, stretching her arms above her head as she yawned, and angry though she was, Beth thought how beautiful the girl looked, flushed and ruffled from sleep and with her lissom body showing clearly through her flimsy nightgown. She thought back momentarily to the previous evening and then drove the memory from her head. No, she was not going to weaken. The girl had to be taken in hand.

When Celeste returned from the bathroom, Beth was sitting on the bed waiting for her. Celeste had thrown cold water onto her face, but still wore only the nightgown.

'Celeste, do you remember what I told you last night?' Beth asked, and if Celeste detected a coldness in her tone, she ignored it.

'Only that I looked beautiful with my head between your legs,' the younger girl replied mischievously.

'No,' Beth said with asperity. 'I told you that you're a lazy good-for-nothing who deserves to have her bottom smacked.'

Celeste pouted. 'What have I done now?'

'Nothing,' Beth said. 'That's just the point. Abso-bloody-lutely nothing... as usual.'

'But there's nothing for me to do,' Celeste complained, and turned away looking for her clothes.

'There's lots for you to do,' Beth retorted. 'Clean the flat, for a start. Get a job, so you can pay your share of the rent.'

'Oh that,' Celeste said dismissively.

Beth exploded. 'Yes, that,' she said, raising her voice. 'Am I going to teach you a lesson now.' She reached out to grasp Celeste's arm and to pull her over her lap, but the girl twisted away.

'You're not going to spank me,' she said emphatically.

Beth began to pursue her. 'Oh yes I am. And hard, with the hairbrush if I can find it in this mess.'

Beth closed on Celeste and the two girls started struggling, at first standing and then falling onto the bed. Try as she might Beth could not get the girl to twist onto her stomach. Although the younger, Celeste was her equal in strength. They fought, pulling each other's hair, pinching and twisting, each crying out in pain. Months of frustration drove Beth on; she was determined to get the upper hand. She was so intent on conquering Celeste, twisting her arm up her back, that at first she did not hear the doorbell.

But eventually the insistent ringing did penetrate their

concentration, shrieking, squealing and panting. Beth left the gasping Celeste on the bed, stomped down the short hall, and threw open the front door. Richard Cross stood on the step, an uneasy smile on his face.

'I thought I would catch you unawares,' he said. 'I imagined we could have part two here in privacy, but judging by the noise I could hear just now I've come at the wrong time.'

'Oh no, on the contrary, Richard,' Beth said, still trying to get her breath back and reaching for his arm. 'You've turned up exactly at the right moment. Come in.'

Leaving Celeste in the bedroom in ignorance about their visitor, Beth led Richard into the sitting room. She was in no mood to beat about the bush.

'Richard, perhaps we could postpone my part two for a while. But I could offer you a part one and a half instead. I have another very suitable candidate for the Richard Cross school of discipline.'

He cocked an interested eyebrow. 'Then I'm at your service.'

'It's Celeste, my flatmate,' Beth went on to explain. 'I was trying to spank her just now but she's a deceptively slippery little madam. She needs to be taught a lesson for being such a lazy little bitch, and I certainly learned a lot yesterday, Richard.'

'Indeed,' he mused. 'So you want me to spank her, or to help you spank her? Is that the idea?'

'I want you to teach her a lesson,' Beth qualified.

'Teach *who* a lesson?' Celeste stalked into the sitting room. She had thrown a dressing gown over her brief nightie but was still barefoot.

Beth introduced them. 'So you're Richard Cross,' Celeste said. There was no polite warmth in her voice but she looked a little less defiant.

'Richard has agreed to help me discipline you,' Beth announced.

'You touch me and I'll sue you for assault,' Celeste warned, but her rebelliousness was clearly ebbing by the second.

'Then we'll have to give you something to sue about,' said Richard, in a tone that invited no argument. He turned to Beth. 'I think she should be completely naked.'

'Don't you dare,' Celeste advised insolently.

'Either you take your clothes off, or we do it for you,' Richard said, and the last spark of Celeste's insubordination was doused. She looked beseechingly at each of them in turn, and then shrugged and slowly took off the dressing gown. She looked up hopefully but Beth saw Richard shake his head, so she lifted her nightdress off completely and stood naked before them, her hands to her sides.

She was as beautiful as any model, even with ruffled hair and without make-up. Her legs were long and slim and her breasts, although on the small side, were beautifully shaped with pink nipples that invited kisses.

But the attention of Richard was between her thighs. She was devoid of hair, looking even more naked than the rest of her as a result. Her labia were clearly visible, pink and private and lusciously inviting. Celeste noticed his eyes, for she looked down at herself.

'I shaved there,' she said with a nervous giggle. 'I wanted to see what it would be like.'

'Clearly not enough to do to occupy herself,' Beth said shortly, but was suddenly surprised to feel jealous. Celeste was so beautiful, Richard was gazing at the gorgeous creature, and she, Beth, had invited him in and was now feeling jealous of the attention he was paying her cheeky flatmate.

Richard Cross looked around the room. 'I think we'll have you over the arm of the sofa,' he said to Celeste, and she now looked distinctly nervous.

'Will you adopt the position yourself?' Richard asked, with exaggerated courtesy. 'Or do we have to make you?'

Celeste shook her head and walked with a seductive naturalness to the sofa. She lay down over one end, the raised and padded arm beneath her hips. Her bottom was thrust into the air, an irresistible invitation. The cheeks were round and firm, the flesh the colour of ivory touched by the pink of a sunset.

'A cushion, I think,' Richard said to Beth. 'Added comfort for her and added exposure for us.' Beth took one from the sofa and, as Celeste lifted herself, squeezed it between her pelvis and the sofa arm.

'Now open your legs,' Richard said, and Celeste obeyed. 'Perfect.'

Beth, watching him and watching Celeste, had a good idea of the thoughts going through his head. Ten minutes ago he had not even met the teenager and already he was looking at her exposed charms. He could not fail to be greatly aroused, to want to thrust his rampant penis deep inside the willing supplicant, to thrash the beautiful naked bottom offered so sweetly for chastisement. Beth too was moved and more than a little excited by the tableau. She could feel the moistness of her own sex, and wished it was her lying over the arm of the sofa with Richard standing above her.

Without thinking about it, she began to undress, and Richard waited patiently as she stripped down to her pink bra and panties. She was not coming second in any

41

competition, she told herself as she reached back to unhook her bra. Her breasts spilled out, free of their lacy constraints.

Beth knew she had Richard's attention. He had never seen her breasts before and she hoped he was not going to forget them. They were firm and full, jutting proudly.

'Perhaps you would be good enough to hold Celeste's hands,' Richard said, and Beth sat on the sofa and took Celeste's wrists, clamping them firmly together on her thighs. Celeste's fingers burrowed for security between them and pressed against her sex, protected only by the thin panties. Beth gazed longingly at the younger girl's back, her vision ending at the twin mounds of her unprotected buttocks awaiting their punishment.

'Now, I am going to spank you hard,' Richard told Celeste. 'Beth can give me a list of your offences.'

'She's a slattern,' Beth accused. 'She never—'

'Slattern will do for a start.' His right hand swept down and landed with a crack on Celeste's left buttock, lifted again, and struck with equal force on the girl's right cheek.

Celeste squirmed and squealed. 'You brute,' she mumbled into the padded seat of the sofa, her meek protestations muffled by it.

'Oh yes, I'm a brute all right. And you're a slattern.' And again he smacked both cheeks, one after the other. Celeste rocked her hips from side to side, and Beth tightened her grip on the girl's wrists while Richard beat a fierce tattoo on each unprotected, quivering cheek.

When he paused for breath and to rub the palm of his right hand, Beth could see Celeste's bottom was turning a deep, alluring red.

'She hasn't paid her share of the rent,' she told Richard, and as he renewed the punishment she found she was tensing her thighs and rubbing the damp front of her panties against Celeste's twitching fingers in time with the strokes. Celeste ground her hips to the same rhythm, raising her bottom after each strike, inviting the next. With intensifying excitement Beth marvelled at the music and rhythm of Richard's spanking technique. The sounds of a hand striking a bottom and Celeste's yelps were the music, the gentle tensing of her own thighs and movement of her sex, and Celeste's clenching and unclenching buttocks were the beat. Beth wished the music and the beat would last forever.

'No job,' she gasped, speaking while she still had sufficient self-control.

Celeste's bottom was by now a bright scarlet.

Richard changed his position so that he stood between the girl's parted legs. 'You will look for work,' he said. 'And keep looking until you find a job. Won't you,' he barked, sweeping his hand down again.

Celeste shrieked and started rocking her bottom from side to side, rubbing her sex against the cushion on which she lay, and Richard maintained his rain of blows with unerring accuracy until the entire target was the same mottled colour.

When finally he stopped, out of breath and rubbing his palm, all three remained silent for a while, the atmosphere in the room electric.

Beth was the first to move. She stood up and looked down at her flatmate's bottom. She was so moved by what she saw that she dropped to her knees beside the girl and pressed her cheek against a crimson buttock, feeling the searing heat on her own skin. Delicately she licked with a cool tongue over the crests of the twin hills, leaving a glistening trail in her wake.

With her cheek still resting on the warm flesh, she looked up at Richard. 'Now the little minx should thank us in a special way,' she said. She reached out with both hands and undid Richard's trousers and let them fall to the floor. With some difficulty she peeled the stretched waistband of his underpants over his erection, and pulled them down. At the same time Richard stripped off his shirt.

He stood naked before them, his erection rigid and long.

Beth helped Celeste get up from the sofa and to kneel before Richard. 'Now you must thank him,' she decreed, and Celeste obediently leaned forward and took one and then both of Richard's balls into her mouth. She sucked gently on their sack, running her tongue around its creases, while against her tearstained cheek his rigid penis quivered with expectation. Releasing his balls, she ran her tongue up its full length from the sack to the head, sucking it in like a plum and pushing the tip of her tongue into the small hole at its peak. With both of her hands cupping his balls, she began to move her head up and down on his erection, taking into her mouth and throat as much as she could manage, while Richard groaned softly.

As Beth watched, she stripped off her knickers. Finally she could wait no longer. 'Now you must thank me,' she said, gently lifting Celeste's head and steering her back to the way she had been over the arm of the sofa. Beth then positioned herself, lying on her back on the sofa, her legs apart, one foot on its back and the other on the floor.

'No more spanking, please,' said Celeste, before slipping her tongue between the glistening labia in front of her and finding the throbbing nub of flesh they concealed.

Beth, her head propped up against the opposite arm of the sofa, watched Richard, standing between Celeste's parted legs, lay his penis in the valley between the girl's red buttocks. With his hands he pushed the mounds together so that only the head was visible pointing at Beth like the muzzle of a rifle.

Celeste moaned and ground her tongue against Beth's clitoris, lapping at it like a kitten with the cream. Through misty eyes Beth watched Richard. Letting go of Celeste's bottom, he guided the florid tip of his penis to her tiny anus, so exposed and inviting beneath him, and nudged against it, as if seeking entry. Celeste moaned again, lifted her bottom and thrust her tongue deep into Beth's vagina, rolling it around the soft muscular walls.

For the first time Richard touched Celeste's hairless and very naked sex, running his penis up and down the wet lips until, with one dramatic thrust of his hips, he penetrated the girl to the hilt.

For Beth time stood still. Nothing mattered but the giving or the receiving of pleasure. Their movements were syncopated – eyelids closing, buttocks and hips grinding, and tongue and cock thrusting in and out. Three as one, reaching for a pinnacle that would not be denied.

So in tune were they that they climbed the mountain and crested its peak together, exploding in and on each other with groans and gasps, then tensed muscles relaxed in replete warmth, and racing blood slowly resumed its more sedate pace.

Chapter Four

Beth enjoyed herself the next morning, getting ready for her meeting with T. J. Kearns. Bathed and powdered, she stood naked before her full length mirror in her bedroom, inspecting herself closely.

'Don't worry, you'll do perfectly.' Celeste was sitting up in the bed they had shared, leaning against a pillow but still sleepy-eyed.

Beth turned around and craned her head back, trying to see the reflection of her bottom. 'Do I still have obvious marks?' she asked, backing up to the bed so the girl could get a closer look.

Celeste stretched out a languid hand and trailed it over Beth's buttocks, sending a shiver up her spine. 'Not too bad at all,' she said. 'Just enough left to make it that bit more interesting.'

'What is it about bottoms that so turns men on?' Beth mused, really enjoying the touch of the younger girl. 'I always thought they were for sitting on.'

'Oh, I can understand,' Celeste said dreamily. 'And yours is really beautiful… beautiful and rude.' As she spoke she cheekily pressed a finger between the lovely cheeks and eased it down and forward to Beth's soft labia. 'How about it?' she whispered, letting her fingertip tease.

Trying not to show her reluctance, Beth tore herself away. 'Oh no, I'm saving myself for whatever is expected of me today,' she said, her voice almost giving away her degree of arousal, and then she took so long trying on clothes and discarding them that Celeste lost interest, got sulkily out of bed, and wandered off to make coffee.

Feeling provocative and incredibly mischievous, Beth chose carefully before finally deciding. Over her white suspender belt, panties and bra, she put on a white blouse that encased her breasts snugly, and a short, dark blue pleated skirt that cinched her waist enticingly. Sitting on the edge of the bed, she then smoothed on a pair of silk stockings and slipped her feet into elegant black shoes.

Standing in front of the mirror again, she surveyed her image with satisfaction. Smart, fashionable, and *very* sexy, with a hint of innocent schoolgirl for anyone who chose to interpret it that way...

Then it was time for her hair; a simple ponytail, her hair pulled back and emphasising her youth and her wide-eyed appeal.

Celeste chose that moment to walk in carrying a cup of coffee for her. 'God, you look gorgeous!' she enthused.

From the looks she attracted from men in the street, Beth knew she had chosen wisely. She received a gratifying look from Jim Tyson, too, who was on his way out as she walked through the lobby of the Rybix building. He raised a questioning eyebrow, but Beth simply smiled and walked on to the reception desk.

'I'm here to see Mr Kearns,' she announced.

The receptionist looked at a list on the desk in front of her and told her to go straight up. Alone in the lift, Beth checked her reflection in the mirror on one wall and held crossed fingers up in front of her face. When the doors opened she was pleased to see there was no sign of Mrs Woods. Kearns himself was opening the double doors to his office – the receptionist had obviously called up to inform of her arrival.

'Ah, Beth,' he said, welcoming her again to his inner sanctum. 'You look… delicious. Absolutely delicious.' He closed the doors. 'Mrs Woods has gone to lunch… a long lunch.'

She sat in the same chair as the previous day, in front of his desk, realising that her skirt, on sitting, was showing a great deal of her stockinged thighs. She surreptitiously eyed his desk for a sign of the contract.

'Let me get you a drink,' he said, staring at her thighs. 'After all, it is lunchtime,' he added.

She accepted a spritzer while he had a large whiskey. She leant back in her chair, sipping her drink and wondering exactly what he had in mind for her. He resumed his position of authority behind the desk and placed his glass on its uncluttered and polished surface. 'Now…' he pondered, his eyes crawling blatantly over her lovely face, down to the white blouse, tight and smooth across her breasts, and back up to her face, '…where were we?'

'The contract,' Beth replied, trying not to transmit her eagerness to secure the deal.

'Ah yes, the contract.' He opened a drawer and withdrew a folder. 'I have it here,' he said. 'But first there is the question of your cooperation.'

Beth looked at him with wide eyes. 'I'm here, aren't I?'

Kearns nodded. 'That's the first step, yes. But there was something else, wasn't there.' He paused, letting his eyes drop again, this time down to her thighs and the teasing skirt. His eyes lifted once more. 'The marks,' he said. 'I had hoped I was going to inspect them again.'

'And I had hoped,' Beth countered, 'that I was going to inspect the company names on the contract.'

'You're very direct for someone who has so much at stake,' Kearns observed. 'I'll give you a clue. At the moment, the company on the contract has the initials C, C and D.'

Beth smiled. 'Perhaps I am too direct; I told you I was naughty. May I have a peek?'

He handed her the contract and there it was, in black and white: Cross, Carstairs and Denton. Three years at six hundred thousand a year. Beth realised it was the moment of decision.

She stood up, placed the folder on the desk, and then walked around to the other side so that she faced Kearns as he swung his chair away from the desk. She stood in front of him, her head cocked slightly to one side.

'I've been very forward and cheeky, sir,' she confessed. 'You said I needed to be taken in hand.'

'You have been very bad,' he said.

She nodded, and her ponytail swayed with the movement. 'Yes sir,' she said, 'and I deserve to be punished. I am so naughty I am always being punished.'

When he spoke his voice was thick. 'No more than you deserve, I've no doubt,' he stated. 'So now I am going to spank you until your bottom is cherry-red.'

'Oh, not a spanking, sir,' she whispered huskily. 'Oh, please no.' Then she added, 'You won't spank me too hard, will you, sir? I'm already a little sore.'

'That's for me to decide and for you to accept,' he insisted firmly. 'Over my lap, with you, this instant.'

Kearns settled himself back in his chair, positioning her over his groin. It seemed he was not about to hurry something he had looked forward to so much.

She felt him pull her skirt up her infinitely slowly, tantalising himself, letting the lines of her legs lead him to the goal he sought.

'Oh no – not my bare bottom, please sir,' Beth squealed. 'Oh no.'

'Oh yes,' Kearns said gruffly. 'I need to see those marks to judge just how severe to be with you.'

She felt his interest intensify beneath her, stirring against her hip, and that stirring became a definite pressure as her white panties came into view. He pressed himself against her warmth and she knew she had chosen her clothes wisely, the aphrodisiac effect of the submissive schoolgirl look.

Beth raised her bottom slightly to allow him to ease her panties down a little. His fingers pressed against her flesh as he peeled them back off her buttocks and down her thighs. She lifted her feet one at a time, so he could take them right off. With her skirt turned up onto her back her bottom was naked – naked and vulnerable... but Kearns was definitely in no hurry.

He trailed his fingers up the back of one thigh to the fading welts on her bottom. 'Such a naughty girl,' he said quietly to himself. He pulled at the cheeks of her bottom to inspect her anus, and then pushed her thighs apart with his hands and tickled her moist sex lips, his fingers tracing their soft dampness.

'Such a very naughty girl,' he repeated, with greater emphasis. And with that he smacked her once. Beth let out a little squeal. She had not expected such force. His palm must have printed itself on her soft flesh, a red map in the shape of a hand on one white buttock. He smacked her again and again, a flurry of smacks, the work of an artist putting the first wash of colour over the canvas.

Beth wriggled and the tendons in her shapely legs tightened as she absorbed the pain. 'I-I promise I'll b-be good, sir,' she stammered, the insistent lump against her hip increasing noticeably. His arousal contributed to hers and she just knew the moistness of her sex was perceptible. Then almost as if he could read her thoughts, Kearns stopped spanking her briefly and inserted one finger between her labia, sliding it back and forth against her clitoris, but Beth's moans of pleasure turned to squeals of protest as he removed his finger and resumed the spanking.

This time there were more controlled pauses between each smack, and each was carefully positioned until both cheeks had been covered from the first sculptured rising sweep at the small of her back to the junction with her thighs.

By the time he stopped again her whole bottom was on fire. With his right hand Kearns lifted her slightly off his lap, and slid his left hand under her stomach. She felt his finger burrow through her pubic hair and insinuate into her sex, the base of the finger against her eager clitoris and the tip inside her vagina. She wiggled her thighs and the sore cheeks of her bottom to allow him easier access and then pushed herself down onto the invading digit.

With his finger satisfactorily in place he resumed the spanking, beating her uncompromisingly with his right palm, the hand almost bouncing, springing up of its own accord from the resilient flesh after each stroke before he swept it down again with a crack of flesh upon flesh. Beth squealed constantly, writhing with increasing abandon on the intrusive finger. Both punisher and punished were totally absorbed in their part of the negotiations.

Then, just as Beth felt her climax was inevitable, Kearns stopped. She could hear him panting as he surveyed his handiwork. Gone were the fading marks on Beth's bottom, and in their place was mottled pink and purple flesh, flaming hot and tender to the touch. Kearns withdrew his finger from her sex and, as she eased herself up from his lap, he began to unfasten his trousers.

'Hold on, T.J.,' Beth spoke between gasps. Her skirt had fallen back into place, but strands of hair stuck to her flushed brow and her cheeks were almost as red as her bottom. 'A spanking, yes, but no one said anything about more than that. What sort of a girl do you think I am?'

Kearns looked stern, but he stopped what he was doing, his waistband undone and his fingers poised on his zip. He glanced at the folder on his desk, and his look said enough.

Beth had another decision to make… she reached for the folder and took an ornate fountain pen out of its holder. She pushed them both to Kearns.

'Five years,' she said unsteadily.

'At five per,' he replied.

'You'll keep it at six if you want my undivided attention,' she replied.

Kearns pondered the deal for a brief moment, and then smiled grimly. He recouped what he could. 'I want you naked first. Completely naked.'

Beth said nothing, but undid her skirt and let it drop to the floor alongside her discarded knickers. It was followed by her blouse, and then her bra, her breasts spilling free before his appreciative gaze.

'You can leave your stockings, suspenders and shoes on,' he told her. 'Now walk to the door and back.'

Beth did as he said, walking very slowly away from him, placing one foot in front of the other so that her punished buttocks jiggled and swung from side to side as she moved. At the door she posed coyly for him, and then returned, her full breasts swaying as her buttocks had done.

'The contract,' she said, once back at the desk. Kearns found the referred to clause in the document and made the agreed changes in ink. 'Initial it,' Beth said.

He did so without a word, and then sat back in his chair, waiting for her to proceed. Beth dropped to her knees in front of him and finished undoing his trousers, and gasped as she pulled down his underpants and took out his penis. What it lacked in length it certainly made up in width. She nuzzled it between her soft breasts, pressing them together with her hands so that it was surrounded by her warm and giving flesh. She rocked slowly up and down as Kearns leaned back in his chair and closed his eyes, his fingers in her hair. After a minute or two, as his breathing became faster, she felt his hands pressing her head down. She wondered if her mouth could encompass his organ, and knew she would enjoy the challenge.

She moistened it first with her tongue, licking around the head and then up and down the shaft. When it was wet enough she stretched her lips wide and slid her mouth over the tip and down its length. It was a tight fit, filling her mouth and nudging into her throat. As she breathed through her nose she let her tongue do the work, licking and sucking simultaneously, slowly at first and then with an increased tempo.

She knew it would not be long. Kearns twisted his fingers in her hair, telling her that she was a bad, bad girl, and how next time he would stick his great cock in her naughty bottom. With every word Beth twirled her tongue around the purple helmet of his penis, faster and faster, gasping for air through her nose as the saliva flooded her mouth. With one hand she grasped his balls and with the other she stroked a line from his anus to his scrotum, leading a path to her lips. Kearns tensed, moaned softly, and ejaculated deep in her throat, a spurt of warm fluid that had travelled far and at speed. Beth just had time to swallow with some difficulty before the second ejaculation shot into her mouth, as warm and salty sticky as before but with less velocity. She eased back a little, but continued to lick the purple head until it had finished its emissions and shrunk back into its foreskin.

Both were dressed and sitting in their respective chairs when they heard Mrs Woods enter the outer room.

Beth held the folder on her lap. 'You know, T.J.,' she said quietly, 'I would have sucked you off even if you didn't change the contract. So long as the contract is ours, I wouldn't have left you like that.'

Kearns chuckled, enjoying a private joke. 'I shouldn't tell you this,' he said, 'but I was lying to you yesterday. You were going to get the contract anyway. I just wanted to see what you would do, how far you would go.'

Walking her to the door, Kearns put his arm around her. 'You're quite a girl, Beth. You wouldn't like a job here, I suppose, working for me?'

'Thanks, but no thanks,' she declined. 'I'm happy where I am; I really like it there.' Then, as an afterthought she added, 'I might know someone who would, though.'

Kearns raised an eyebrow: 'Someone like you?' he said suggestively.

'Someone just as naughty as me, if that's what you mean. In fact, she's even naughtier. She needs a firm hand, the smack of real discipline.' Beth opened the door. 'I might arrange for her to come and see you.'

In the anteroom, she handed the folder to Mrs Woods. 'Photocopy this, please,' she said. 'Type it up again from the photocopy. I'll take the original with me. You can fax the amendments later.'

'This is the second present I've given you,' Beth said, handing the folder to Richard Cross. It was six-thirty and they were again alone in his office.

Richard studied the contract long and hard, and then closed the folder with a low whistle of appreciation. 'I like the alterations made in pen.'

Beth smiled coquettishly. 'I thought you would,' she said with pride, and threw herself down on the sofa, flipping her legs up onto the cushions.

'It will do wonders for the next set of figures,' Richard said. 'How did you do it? T.J. isn't easy.'

She laughed. 'Sacrifice far beyond the call of duty.'

'Sacrifice? What sort of sacrifice? Nothing painful, I hope.'

She gave him a look full of meaning. 'I suspect you'll find out for yourself fairly soon.'

He looked puzzled briefly, and then changed the subject. 'Five or six months from now I'll have to think again about carrots instead of sticks. What would you like?'

'I'll have to think about it,' Beth teased. 'I'll let you know.'

Richard nodded. 'You said it was today's second present. What was the first?'

'Don't tell me you've forgotten Celeste already,' she said indignantly.

He smiled at the recollection. 'Oh yes, Celeste. Of course.'

Beth swung her feet to the floor. 'Did you enjoy spanking her?'

Richard leaned back in his chair, a smile playing about

his lips. 'Yes,' he said thoughtfully. 'I did, very much.'

'As much as caning me?' asked Beth, and immediately regretted the note of jealousy that crept into her voice.

Richard heard it and was not going to let her off the hook. 'Different circumstances,' he said. 'Different situation.'

'A different bottom, too,' Beth said, pouting. 'You preferred her to me.'

'I didn't say that.'

'You didn't need to,' Beth sulked. 'You fucked her, but you didn't even touch me.'

'Is that wise?' Richard said, his expression and tone suddenly grim.

'Is what wise?'

'Getting all possessively broody on me, the man who is about to punish you.'

'You... you're still going to punish me after all I've done for you today?' she blurted indignantly.

'Oh yes,' Richard confirmed. 'Isn't that what you're here for?'

'Is Celeste not enough for you?' she said, secretly pleased that her flatmate had not drained his libido.

'I can handle more than one naughty girl in a day,' he stated. 'Speaking of which...' his voice dropped the bantering tone, '...I'd like you naked – now.'

Without question Beth stood and started to undress, without being self-conscious, as if she was alone in her bedroom, folding each garment neatly on the sofa. When she was totally naked she walked around the desk and posed in front of him, standing straight with one arm across her breasts and her other hand on her pubis.

Richard looked into her eyes. 'Move your hands,' he said, so she dropped them to her sides, standing quietly as he looked her up and down, slowly and carefully. She searched his eyes for a look of approval, but then he commanded her to turn around.

She heard him whistle softly and she knew why; her bottom was pink all over and purple in parts, still showing the effects of the last two days.

'That's not all my handiwork,' he said, a note of admiration in his voice.

'No, it's not,' Beth confirmed, still standing with her back to him. 'I had a top up at lunchtime.'

'A top up?'

He was being obtuse. 'All part of securing the deal,' Beth informed him.

Richard chuckled. 'Well, well, T.J. you old dog. I never would have guessed.' He reached for her arm and pulled her gently across his lap. 'Such dedication to duty, my dear,' he said with evident approval. 'Keep it up and you'll go far in this company. I must take a close look at your work.'

Beth lay contentedly over his thighs as he gently stroked her bottom, running his fingers across the warm, slightly swollen flesh, and she felt disappointed when she heard him say, 'I won't punish you again tonight. We must give these…' and he lightly tapped her buttocks, '…a proper chance to recover.'

With deepening disappointment she thought he was going to make her rise and send her home, but then she felt a finger tickling the entrance to her sex, sliding smoothly up and down the outer lips, lubricated by the moisture she had unwittingly generated. She was still stimulated, and unsatisfied, from her appointment with Kearns, and she knew she would quickly come under Richard's control and touch.

'You are a beautiful girl, Beth, made to be loved and punished,' he said huskily. 'Made for my satisfaction.' As he spoke his finger penetrated between the lips of her sex and slid easily into the warm moistness inside. She hardly heard his words; his finger was so much more expressive. She moaned softly and gently pushed herself against his hand. He withdrew the finger and ran it slowly in a circular motion around the taut nub of her clitoris.

'My satisfaction,' he repeated. 'I am not going to spank you this evening, but I am going to punish you in a way.' Panting slightly, she began to rotate her haunches in time with his finger. 'I am going to penetrate you,' he went on. 'I am going to come inside you.' She moaned with yearning as she ground her cunt hard against his hand. 'But you are forbidden to have a climax,' he declared. 'That is your punishment.'

In the confusion of her euphoria, the meaning of his words took a second or two to dawn on her. Then with an audible groan she pushed back as if she wanted all his hand in her sex. She was just seconds away, rushing to catch a train which, cruelly, pulled away just as she was reaching for the door.

She felt like crying with frustration, and spoke for the first time since she had lain across his lap. 'But that's just not fair, Richard,' she protested pitifully. 'Please, please don't be so cruel.'

But he was implacable. 'You have to be punished, my dear, and this is tonight's punishment. You must pleasure me, but not yourself.' He was stroking her buttocks again. 'Where would you like me? In your beautiful mouth? In here?' and he tormented her clitoris with his finger, reminding her yet again just how close she had been. 'Or in here...?'

The finger, still moist from her excitement, pushed its way between the cheeks of her bottom and began stroking the rosebud of her anus. 'It's your choice,' she heard him say. 'But whichever way you choose, you are forbidden to climax.'

Her excitement began to mount again. His finger slowly and gently penetrated the tight circle. It was not to be denied.

'Are you a virgin here, Beth?' he asked.

She replied with a muffled sound of confirmation, unable to formulate words. At the feel of his finger in her bottom she knew she wanted it to go on, that she wanted nothing more and that she was close again to a climax. She lifted her hips so the finger sank deeper. Never had a man touched her so intimately, so wonderfully, that she could no longer differentiate between the discomfort of it and the pleasure.

'Yes, Richard, in my bottom, please,' she gasped shamefully, unable to help herself.

He immediately withdrew his finger and her tight rear passage, like her sex moments before, suddenly and abruptly felt empty and unloved. Again she slid down the mountain of excitement she had been so rapidly ascending. Again the peak, the climax, was denied her.

'Oh no, my girl,' Richard said, giving her bottom a sharp smack. 'Oh no you don't. You are forbidden to climax, and by being so wanton and greedy you have made up my mind; you will please me with your mouth.' He smacked her bottom again. 'We'll save this little treat for another day.'

So saying, he abruptly pushed her off his lap and she fell at his feet, barely able to control her breathing. She lay panting on the floor, hating him and wanting him simultaneously. He was cruel but she wanted him, and she wanted him to be cruel.

With no further orders she rose unsteadily to her knees, unbuckled his belt, opened his trousers, and rummaged inside for his erection, pulling it out into the open before her flushed face. She gazed longingly at it, admiring its length and rigidity, and beauty – it was an object of worship.

She puckered her lips again and blew warm breath on its florid summit, looking up at his face from under her lowered eyelids. 'This is the rod you would like to beat me with.' He didn't have to answer; the answer was in the organ itself, already erect to bursting it seemed to swell further with pride. 'It is the rod I would like you to use on me, on my bottom... in my bottom.'

She looked at Richard with eyes clouded by lust, then opened her mouth and gently swallowed his tight scrotum, sucking at the balls as if they were sweets and running her warm, unseen tongue around the creases of the sack. She knew he would be gazing at the double curve of her bottom as it disappeared out of his sight, the dimples on her lower back on either side.

Beth ran her tongue from the scrotum up the tall pulsing column to the tip, hesitated slightly and then with an audible, wet plop took the purple head into her mouth. She ran her tongue around the firm edge of the helmet and then lowered her head so that much of his penis disappeared down her warm, wet, inviting throat. Slowly but with increasing speed she moved her lips tightly up and down the quivering organ, lubricating it with saliva as she breathed smoothly through her nose.

They were each in their own way so taken up with what they were doing that they never heard the office door open and soft footfalls on the carpet; it was the voice that disturbed them and made them both jump.

'Working late at the office, I see. You always said you got your best work done in the evening, darling.'

Beth looked up and froze, still with her lips sealed around Richard's penis. A woman stood to his side and slightly behind him, her hand on his shoulder. 'I'm Helen Cross,' she said, and then added unnecessarily, 'Richard's wife.' She held out her hand and then changed her mind, putting it back on Richard's shoulder in a possessive gesture.

'Please don't try to talk with your mouth full,' she said to Beth, as if she was a naughty child at the dinner table. 'You've started, so you may as well finish.'

Beth was dumbstruck. Just as she was about to draw her head away Richard's already swollen penis felt as though it doubled in size, adding to her confusion. If she had a chance to think about it, she would have guessed that it would have gone instantly flaccid at the intrusion, but on the contrary, it seemed to grow. He was actually excited by his wife's presence!

But none of this dawned on Beth in her confusion. She reacted instinctively, and her instinct dictated that she sucked the inflated penis with redoubled vigour, saliva running down its smooth sides.

Helen Cross walked around her kneeling form. 'This must be the naughty Beth Forrester you were telling me about.' She stood behind her. 'And this must be the naughty Miss Forrester's naughty bottom,' she said.

The soft cheeks swayed and bucked a little with each thrust of Beth's head. 'You were right, Richard,' Helen said brightly. 'It is a perfectly delightful bottom, designed for the lash. But how you disappoint me, Richard darling. It is hardly touched, hardly a mark to indicate your pleasure. Where's your office cane, the one I bought you for Christmas?'

Bizarrely, the woman then stooped down behind Beth for a closer inspection, and ran her hand over and around one pink cheek and down into the cleft between.

'I said I wouldn't beat her tonight,' Richard grunted, his voice strained. 'But she is forbidden to have a climax.'

'Absolute rubbish,' his wife said scornfully. 'This isn't a game. This is different. I am angry; I don't like to see naughty girls dining off my husband. I didn't promise not to punish her, so I shall. Where's that cane?'

Richard found it easier to nod than to speak. He indicated the drinks cabinet and watched dumbly as Helen found the cane and returned, cutting it in the air, to stand behind Beth.

She then spoke briskly to the girl whose mouth was full of her husband's erection. 'If we are going to do this right, we must get some rhythm into it.'

As Beth's head bobbed up and down in Richard's lap, Helen raised the cane and, on the down stroke, suddenly lashed the girl's buttocks. Beth had expected it, secretly welcomed it, and did not break her fluid movement, other than to gasp for air on the up stroke. With the next down stroke the cane fell again, biting into the soft flesh, which made Beth all the more eager to swallow yet more of the thrusting penis.

By the third stroke all three participants had synchronised their movements, Richard's hips, Beth's mouth and bottom, and Helen's right arm moved in unison. As Richard began to clench his muscles, indicating he was near to coming, and as the pain of her bottom reached her sex as warm pleasure, Beth realised she was close to a climax herself. She rolled her hips and moaned as she moved her head up and down at an ever-faster rate and the cane maintained the beat.

'This naughty girl is going to defy us,' Helen said, panting slightly and beating yet faster time across Beth's smarting buttocks. 'We forbid you to climax.'

But it was beyond her or anyone's control. Three things happened at once. The cane landed with the cruellest stripe yet, Richard exploded, shooting his warm, sticky fluid deep down the girl's throat, and Beth herself – oh, blessed relief – felt a complementary explosion deep inside herself, starting from her womb and running up to her breasts and down her thighs. She fell limply to the floor, her body quivering and drops of Richard's creamy ejaculation on her lips and chin.

'You disobeyed me!' Helen roared. 'You'll pay for that.' She looked down upon Beth and her anger flared.

'Look at her, Richard.' He opened one eye. 'Look at her. She enjoyed it. She cheated us. She actually got off on me beating her.'

Helen lashed out again with the cane, catching Beth a cruel blow across the back of her thighs just where the moist lips of her sex peeped between. Another smaller paroxysm convulsed Beth's body, the aftershock of the tremors before.

Then the passion of Helen's disturbing anger changed to cold calculation. 'For now,' she announced primly, 'I am going to punish you by not punishing you any more.'

But Beth was past hearing or caring.

Chapter Five

'Why do so many men like to spank a girl's bottom?'
Beth asked. As soon as she had asked the question, though,
she was swamped in confusion. She had not planned to
ask it. It just came out.

The female psychiatrist smiled. The question was
unexpected, but the answer was ready. That was what
being a professional shrink was all about, the quick and
facile answer no matter how surprising or shocking the
question.

'Could it be that they are angry with women?' the
psychiatrist asked.

Beth had started to see Dr Susskind immediately after
her promotion. It was her reward to herself, a status
symbol, a following of fashion. Now that she had a high-
powered, stressful job, did not she, like everyone else in
her shoes, deserve the mandatory weekly session with a
shrink?

That was how it started, but Beth had come to value
their regular sessions. Nothing of much consequence was
said, but Beth learned to enjoy the quiet concentration on
her, and the things that mattered to her, for an hour at a
time, the opportunity to speak only about her free of the
charge of egotism, and the chance to speak her mind and
vent her frustrations. Sixty pounds a time was a small
price to pay for such luxury. With the psychiatrist's gentle
probing, she found the session helped to clear her mind.
They had developed a genuine rapport. At the end of each

hour, Beth had refreshed her sense of priorities. She found she felt better even though she had not necessarily felt bad beforehand.

'Seriously, let me answer your question initially with another question of my own,' the psychiatrist replied. 'Why do you ask? Has someone been spanking your bottom?'

Beth reddened. 'Maybe,' she muttered after a pause.

The psychiatrist leaned forward and switched off the tape recorder on the desk. 'Let me remind you, Beth, that everything we discuss here is confidential. I would not have it any other way. Anything you say will not go beyond these four walls. Now, have you been spanked recently?'

Beth stuck out her lower lip. 'Answer my question first. Why *do* so many men like to spank a girl's bottom?'

Dr Susskind smiled at her determination. 'First it is a question of aesthetics. The female bottom is the most beautiful, the most perfect part of the human anatomy, beloved by sculptors, painters, poets and lechers alike. Secondly, think of where it is situated, of its neighbours. It is the portal to paradise for most males, the entrance to the hidden chambers of pleasure.'

Beth nodded. 'But why spank it? Why not just kiss it, or lick it? Why not love it?'

'That is where aesthetics meet the id, the male id,' the psychiatrist said. 'It is to do with power and dominance. The priapic male is the hunter, the submissive female the victim, the more submissive the better.'

'Oh,' Beth said, disappointment in her voice. 'Is that all it is?'

'Don't underestimate it, Beth,' Dr Susskind said. 'The urge to chastise girls is very strong in the male of the species. It may be a private and personal compunction or pastime but it comes into the open time and time again. You're too young to remember the spanking colonel.'

Beth looked puzzled.

'A few years ago,' the psychiatrist went on, 'some old buffer with a boat on the Thames. He used to entice girls on board and spank their bare bottoms. One silly girl complained. It got tremendous publicity. Everyone loved reading about it. A lot of people could see nothing wrong in what he did.'

Beth giggled.

'And there's Hazlitt. William Hazlitt, the essayist two hundred years ago.' Dr Susskind looked enquiringly and Beth nodded, reminding herself to look up the name later. 'A most respected and respectable man. He was sitting by himself in a meadow in the Lake District, no doubt deep in profound thought, when a pert local village girl went by. He must have been overcome by an irresistible urge. In a trice he had her over his lap with her skirts up and was spanking her bottom. There was quite a scandal. Hazlitt returned to London that night.'

Beth laughed. 'She must have been surprised. I must read Hazlitt.'

'Surprised, no doubt. Hurt, probably. And young, almost definitely.'

'What makes you say that?' Beth asked.

'Only the very young or stupid would make a hullabaloo in a situation like that.'

'What do you mean?' Beth asked, feeling indignant on the girl's behalf. 'He might have hurt her.'

'True,' the psychiatrist said. 'But the first rule of being a female, especially a young and poor female, is that if you have something that a powerful man wants, you don't make a row and scare him away, you milk it for all it's worth. Just think what she might have got out of Hazlitt. Even a few sovereigns at worst would have been better than a scandal, and probably another beating from her father.'

Beth nodded knowingly, encouraging the psychiatrist to continue.

'Think of a word you like,' the psychiatrist said.

'What do you mean?' Beth asked, puzzled.

'Think of a word you like. That you like the sound of, or the meaning of.'

'Lullaby,' Beth said. 'I like lullaby.'

The psychiatrist nodded. 'Lullaby. Yes, that's a pretty word. What does it mean to you?'

'Peace and serenity,' Beth said. 'Love and warmth.'

The psychiatrist nodded again. 'Now think of a word that you find sexy, a turn on.'

Beth thought for a moment. 'Lingerie,' she said, with a giggle. 'Lacy knickers. Suspenders. Low cut bras.'

Dr Susskind smiled and nodded in approval. 'Now can you think of a word that might turn men on, that they find sexy?'

Beth shook her head. 'I honestly have no idea.'

'Spanking,' Dr Susskind said. 'That is a trigger word for many males. Spanking. To spank. A good spanking.' Beth listened wide-eyed as the psychiatrist continued. 'The word turns them on. The thought turns them higher. And the act... ah, the act turns them to white heat.'

'I think I like the sound of it too,' Beth said, blushing slightly. She held her head to one side as if thinking. 'To be given a good spanking,' she said, rolling the words around in her mouth. 'Naughty girls like me deserve to be spanked, and spanked hard.' She flashed a sudden smile at the psychiatrist. 'Yes, I like it too. There is a definite frisson.'

The psychiatrist nodded again. 'The word, and the deed, are perfect for the rampant male. In a punishment situation, the male thinks he has the whip hand. But he hasn't. In reality it is the chastised female who is the powerful one, not the lustful male who seeks nothing but sensual and sexual satisfaction.'

Beth was puzzled. 'Because she has what he wants?'

'Yes, and because she will always have it and he will always want it,' Dr Susskind said. 'If you answer my question I'll let you into a secret.'

'What question?'

'Have you been spanked?'

Beth nodded. 'Yes,' she admitted quietly.

'Recently?'

She nodded again. 'Yesterday. Now what's the secret?'

'It's pretty obvious really, but it is something in my job I know for a fact.' Beth sat forward eagerly, hanging on every word. 'There are far more men in the world who want to spank a girl's bottom than there are girls who want or are prepared to be spanked.'

Dr Susskind saw the disappointed look on Beth's face. 'Think about it; think what it means.'

Beth nodded and was silent for a moment. Then she spoke hesitantly, 'What happens if a girl actually likes it?'

'What happens in what way?' Dr Susskind asked. 'It makes her all the more powerful.'

'But what happens physically? Why should I... why should a girl actually like it?'

Dr Susskind studied the girl for a moment before answering. 'Come over here, Beth. I will show you.'

Almost as if she was mesmerised, Beth found herself getting up. She knew she was incapable of refusing Dr

Susskind; you don't pay sixty pounds an hour and then ignore the instructions or advice. And anyway, Dr Susskind was an imposing, almost frightening woman, twice Beth's age but slender and well groomed, smart of dress and smarter of mind, not someone to be lightly disobeyed.

Dr Susskind pushed her chair back from her desk as Beth approached. 'Slip off your skirt and knickers; we don't want them getting in the way,' she said briskly. 'And don't be shy; we're all girls here. You can keep the rest on, we don't want you getting cold.'

When Beth was naked between the bottom of her short lilac jumper and the top of her stockings, pinched up by suspenders, the psychiatrist patted the desk in front of her. 'Lean over this,' she said. 'Rest your head on it.'

With her head down and her legs straight, Beth's bottom was beautifully presented to the seated psychiatrist. Beth heard her chair creak as the older woman leaned forward and studied it carefully like an unexpected and exotic Christmas present.

'Well,' Dr Susskind said eventually, 'you didn't have to answer my question. I can see you have been both spanked and caned in the last few days.'

Beth nodded, but when she realised the woman might not see the response, she muttered, 'Yes.'

'It must be sore.'

'Yes, it is a little.'

'Open your legs wider,' Dr Susskind said seductively, and Beth obeyed, leaning forward as she did so. At this, she knew the lips of her sex came more into view and she heard the psychiatrist swallow as she studied the beauty so readily presented to her.

'Let me ask you a question,' Dr Susskind said. 'Think carefully before you answer. Did you enjoy it, being spanked and caned?'

For the third time, Beth said yes. 'Not at the time maybe, but soon afterwards.'

'Did you enjoy it very much? So much that it helped you to orgasm?'

'Yes.'

'Did you actually climax while you were being punished?'

'Yes,' for the fifth time.

'You are a very unusual girl. Shall I tell you why – why you enjoyed it?' But before Beth could answer, Dr Susskind held her hips. 'Better still, let me show you.' She gently pulled the girl back and placed her over her lap, and slid one hand between her legs to open them as they had been before.

That moment, as she slipped into place over Dr Susskind's lap, was a timeless one for Beth, one of those moments in life when one is at peace with the world and content with one's place in it. She had been there before, she was there now, and she would be there again in the future. The position was right, the exposure of her most intimate parts to an older, wiser person was right, her total defencelessness was right. The rough tweed of Dr Susskind's skirt tickled her lower belly and tugged gently at her pubic hair. The psychiatrist's fingers lightly caressed the soft, marked flesh of her buttocks. Beth felt the warmth of the older woman's body suffusing her loins, sending messages of lazy comfort to her brain. Her eyes filled with tears, she was so happy. If only this moment of total surrender could last forever.

When Dr Susskind spoke again it was as if her voice came from far away. 'You think it is all to do with this.' As she spoke, Dr Susskind drew a painted fingernail against the moist lips of Beth's sex, and the girl shivered. 'Or even this,' the psychiatrist said, continuing the line of the fingernail up the valley between Beth's buttocks, lingering momentarily on the rosebud so invitingly exposed.

'But it's not, you know.' She slapped Beth's buttocks. 'It's not here, but here.' With her left hand she caressed Beth's hair. 'It's in the mind.'

Dr Susskind pinched one of the bruises on Beth's bottom and Beth squealed lightly, a squeal that became a sigh.

'When you're hurt, when anyone is hurt, the brain reacts to protect the body. It releases what we call endorphins, a natural opiate that acts as a painkiller. If you had ever taken morphine you would recognise it, a warm feeling that nothing could ever hurt you again.'

As she spoke, Dr Susskind was stroking Beth's body from the backs of her knees to her waist. Beth nestled deeper into her lap.

'In your case, Beth, from what you say, your brain works even better than most, releasing more endorphins than you need. It is not unheard of, but it is rare. You are one of those lucky people who actually feel better after being hurt. And because you are young, healthy and sexy, your body translates that feeling sexually. You get the feeling others get when they make love.'

Dr Susskind trailed the fingers of her right hand up and down the cleft of Beth's bottom. 'From what you say,' she went on, 'in your case it goes as far as giving you an orgasm. I have never heard of that before, but I am prepared to believe it. We all live and learn. If it is true, I might write a paper on it.'

'I think it is true,' Beth said, her voice muffled.

'Let's conduct an experiment,' Dr Susskind said. 'I shall slap you and I want you to tell me what you feel.'

71

Beth whispered her assent, and Dr Susskind leaned forward and kissed her mouth-watering bottom, running her tongue over the silken skin, tasting the soft flesh. 'You have such a beautiful bottom, my dear.' Beth could feel the woman's warm breath fanning her nakedness. 'It seems a shame to hurt it, but science calls...'

She slapped the pliant bottom in front of her with all the strength she could muster.

Beth gasped and bucked on her lap, but Dr Susskind held her in place with a lightly restraining hand. 'Tell me what you feel.'

Beth paused. 'It hurt... now it's warm... it feels nice... very nice.'

As Beth spoke, she knew her buttocks were reddening and the lips of her sex relaxing, exposing the moist pinkness within. Dr Susskind leaned closer and blew warm air across her labia.

When the psychiatrist spoke again, her voice was thick with a passion she was trying unsuccessfully to suppress. 'It seems to work. Shall we try for the jackpot? Do you think you could climax like that?'

'With you, yes,' Beth said. 'Will you spank me, please?'

It lasted a long time, their game, a game with unspoken rules, a serious game that neither wanted to end. Dr Susskind did nothing but spank Beth, she touched her in no other way, but the spanking was careful and deliberate, measured to a fine degree. Initially each slap was hard but well apart, at least thirty seconds between blows to allow each to have its full effect. At each Beth moaned, but it was not a moan of hurt or complaint, but more a reply, an acknowledgement of what the other had done, and she would raise her buttocks for the next slap.

When the bottom on her lap was a bright crimson all

72

over and fiercely warm to the touch, Dr Susskind stepped up the pace with light, flicking slaps, each hard on the heels of the last. Beth's moans ran into each other, a long, low, gurgling cry of ecstasy seeking an outlet. She had hands pressed to the floor for support as her lower body writhed and twisted, always presenting itself.

The third and final stage, when it came, was a flurry of flesh on flesh and the sound of blood pulsing in the ears. The world outside was lost; all that existed were the two of them and what was happening there and then. Dr Susskind rained blow after blow on the receptive target, apparently unaware of the pain in her hand. Beth knew, and she knew it was obvious to Dr Susskind too, that she was going to orgasm. Her gasps were rising in pitch, and her bottom was writhing up and down, her labia opening and dripping with moisture like a flower trying to attract a humming bird. Dr Susskind panted as she thrashed faster and harder. Beth began a scream. 'Yes,' she cried. 'Oh yes. Oh yes… yesss.' The storm broke. Her thighs and buttocks clenched and unclenched until finally she laid still, her breath slowly returning to normal.

When she sat up and eased herself off Dr Susskind's lap, she had tears in her eyes. 'Oh my,' she gasped, 'it has never been like that.'

Leaning her sore and still naked bottom on the edge of the desk, she took Dr Susskind's flushed cheeks in her hands and kissed her on the lips. 'Thank you,' she said. 'Thank you so much. I wish there was something I could do for you.' She picked up Dr Susskind's right hand, the hand that had given her so much pleasure, and kissed and gently licked the tingling palm.

Dr Susskind looked embarrassed. 'I am glad it was so successful but you must excuse me,' she said. 'I find I was not unmoved by the experience. It's most unprofessional. I won't be long.'

She rose from her seat, apparently heading for the lavatory just to the side of her office. Beth was a little slow on the uptake, but not that slow. 'Are you going to do what I think?' she asked, wondering why she was being so coy. They were both being coy, after what had happened.

Dr Susskind's expression was sufficient answer, so Beth took her by the hand. 'Let me help. It's the least I can do. I want to.'

She led the unresisting Dr Susskind to the couch, the psychiatrist's couch they had both laughed about. Gently and slowly she undressed the older women, marvelling at the beauty she preserved, the girlishness of her underwear and her figure once the professional suiting was removed. She removed the bra and then knelt down and eased off her knickers, and could smell the women's desire. She rubbed her nose into the soft pubic hair in front of her. 'I don't even know your first name,' she muttered.

The psychiatrist giggled guiltily. 'It's Eunice, but I don't like it. My friends call me Tip, but it's a long story.'

Beth pushed her back so that she sat on the coach. 'Well Tip, this is for you.' She eased the woman back, parted her thighs, and then squatted between her legs, her still naked, hot bottom resting on her heels, the warmth of Tip's thighs against her shoulders.

Now she could taste the desire. She ran the tip of her tongue up and down, darting in and out of her vagina, before settling on the firm, surprisingly large bud. She could feel Tip's hands in her hair, grasping her head on either side and holding her close. Without letting go of the clitoris between her lips, she raised her hand and inserted one finger, and then two, into the moist warmth alongside her chin. The fingers delved as deeply as possible before rotating against the muscular walls as Beth sucked and licked with increasing intensity.

It did not last long. The psychiatrist needed little encouragement or assistance. Within seconds, it seemed, she was roughly grinding Beth's head into her loins, so hard that it was uncomfortable where the pubic bone of the one met the upper lip of the other. Beth could hardly breathe. The climax arrived like an express train, announced by a loud, unladylike scream and an ever-tighter grip on Beth's hair. Beth was not so taken up with what she was doing that she didn't have time to marvel at it. She thought only men ejaculated. She wondered if she did herself. She knew she became very wet, but to ejaculate... she would have to ask Celeste, at an appropriate moment of course.

Dr Susskind pushed her head away. 'No more,' she said breathlessly. 'I can't take any more.'

Five minutes later, breathing more normally, the two took it in turns to use the bathroom, to comb their hair and to adjust their clothes.

Then there was an uncomfortable moment of unreal formality. Standing by the door, Tip Susskind kissed Beth briefly on the cheek. 'Thank you, Beth,' she said. 'Same time next week?' She blushed. 'Perhaps we can resume our researches then. Such an interesting topic, and there is so much more to learn.'

Beth kissed the psychiatrist on the lips. 'If we are going to resume our researches,' she said, 'perhaps we should reverse the fee structure, not me paying you but you paying...'

Beth could see that Dr Susskind was about to

expostulate, and interrupted herself. 'Look at it this way, Tip,' she said hastily. 'If you pay me then you'll know, we'll both know, know for a fact, that I am a naughty girl, a very bad girl. And bad girls have to be punished, don't they?'

'I can see why you do so well in business, Beth,' Dr Susskind said. 'We might come to some sort of an arrangement.'

Beth took Tip's right hand and raised it to her mouth, again kissing the sore palm, still red and smarting from the spanking it had delivered.

'Let's face it, Tip,' she murmured. 'You enjoyed spanking me. Admit it. Be honest, wouldn't you like to do it again, and soon?'

Walking back to the office through Parliament Square, Beth considered that she had never felt happier than she did at that moment. She was happy and it showed. Her eyes were bright, her cheeks pink, her step was light and her stride easy. Her hips and her hair swayed in unison with each step.

Beth knew from experience that even at her worst moments she was a woman that men looked at, and looked at again. She was pretty enough, but today she was radiant too. Hardly a man passed her without looking her up and down with faraway longing in their eyes. She knew without looking herself that many looked back at her to see her from behind.

Dream on you poor sods, Beth thought. How you'd love to see my bottom bare, to smack it with your hands, a slipper, or a cane. She giggled. If only you knew you probably could. I would probably let you. And what's more, I would probably love it. She smiled happily.

76

Chapter Six

The morning sun streaming through the windows woke Beth early. It was Saturday. No work. She sat up in bed, refreshed and happy, glad to see the day and still with the warm feeling of well being from the previous afternoon. The office had been empty when she returned; people in her business were used to getting away to the country early on Fridays. She had been quietly pleased that Richard had gone. She felt she'd taken all the punishment she could for a while, and was doubly pleased when she returned home to find it empty for the evening. Beth liked her solitude at times and the chance for the self-indulgence of mudpacks and manicures.

Celeste's tousled head lay on the pillow next to her. What a cheek, Beth thought, to get into her bed uninvited. At the same time she was touched that Celeste felt sufficiently fond of her and at ease that she would want to share her bed just for sleeping. Beth pushed back the duvet and gazed at the younger girl who was lying on her stomach, naked.

She was truly beautiful. The word pneumatic came into Beth's mind. There was not a wrinkle or mark on Celeste's soft skin, it was as if the girl had been inflated like a balloon. In studying paintings or photographs of nudes, Beth had always preferred the male figure, the sharp angles and muscular planes. The female figure was too curved and rounded, and therefore uninteresting. But looking at Celeste now she could see how beautiful a female could be, and how desirable she would be to any man. Who wouldn't want to fuck her? For a moment Beth felt quite jealous of men and their penises.

Celeste stirred and reached for the duvet. Beth leaned over and kissed the nape of her neck, where her hair brushed her shoulders. 'You make the coffee,' she whispered. 'I'm going to have a shower. I want to talk to you.'

Half an hour later they were back in bed, still naked but showered and powdered, leaning back against pillows and sipping coffee. 'Don't you just love Saturdays?' Celeste asked, tickling Beth's foot with her toes.

Beth snorted. 'I don't see that weekends make any difference to you. You never work.'

Celeste made a moue of protest. 'But I have you on weekends.'

'You would enjoy them more if you had a job,' Beth said. 'That's what I want to talk to you about. I think I may have found you one.'

Celeste's 'Oh?' was distinctly unenthusiastic.

'It could be a good job, a great job,' Beth said fiercely, trying to get Celeste to snap out of her lassitude. She told her about Rybix, mentioning Kearns but giving few details.

Celeste put down her cup and turned to face Beth. 'But I don't have any experience.'

Beth looked at her. 'You don't have many qualifications either. But you have your looks, a sharp brain and an even sharper tongue. You should learn to use them.'

'Oh pooh,' Celeste said, and snuggled deeper into the bed.

'You won't get any experience if you don't get a job,' Beth went on. 'You should be prepared to use whatever skills and talents you have just to get a job in the first place, and then learn and learn.'

'What skills? What talents?' Celeste's tone was truculent.

'Your looks and your wits,' Beth said. 'How did you feel the other day, with Richard?'

'Excited,' Celeste admitted. 'He's a good-looking man.'

'Did you mind when he spanked you?'

'Not at all – I quite liked it. And anyway, you were there.'

'There you are then,' Beth said, as if her argument was won. 'You did that and there was nothing in it for you.' Celeste cocked an eyebrow, but Beth went on. 'How would you feel if another man spanked you, and say I wasn't there?'

'I suppose it depends what he was like. Some older men can be quite attractive. Just so long as they don't have beer bellies and hair growing out of their ears.' Celeste shrugged her naked shoulders. 'It could be okay, I suppose – in theory, at least. It depends.' She thought for a moment, and then became indignant. 'Hey, is that the job, being spanked by strange men?'

'No,' Beth replied. 'Not necessarily. It could be a good job, you could probably define your own role, but you should be prepared to… let's just say, you should be prepared to use what assets you have to your own advantage.'

Celeste studied her friend. 'Would you do it?' she asked.

Beth laughed. 'I find I am doing it. Against my choosing, but you'd be amazed at how effective it is. I've learned a lot in the last few days.'

'Doing what, exactly?'

'Using my talents to their full, shall we say. I've found recently that I have talents I didn't know I had.'

Celeste's 'Hmmm' made her sound unconvinced, so

Beth went on. 'I went to see Dr Susskind yesterday. She taught me something I didn't know about myself. Being spanked can actually turn me on. So why shouldn't I use it to my advantage? Can I help it if my bottom is as important as my brain.'

'I think I know what you mean,' Celeste said. 'I can remember the first time it happened to me. I was quite young and I was caned. It was a tremendous turn on.'

'Funny you should say that,' Beth interjected. 'When I was with Dr Susskind yesterday I remembered something from the past, my first time, something I had totally forgotten. I was lying over her lap…'

Celeste exploded. 'You were lying over her lap? Dr Susskind's lap? Was she spanking you?'

'Yes,' Beth continued, unruffled. 'I was lying over her lap and it suddenly all came flooding back. It was a weird but very comforting feeling. It felt right, and everything fell into place.'

Celeste put her arm around Beth's shoulders. 'Tell Mother Celeste. I want to hear all about it.'

'I'll tell you about my first time, if you'll tell me about yours,' Beth said. 'But before we change the subject, I want you to promise me something. If I make an appointment for you at Rybix about a job, you'll go and you'll do your very best even if, at first, not everything is entirely to your taste.'

'You'll be with me?' Celeste asked.

'Yes, if that's what you'd like,' Beth said, and then added, 'For the first time only, though.'

'Okay then,' Celeste decided, after a moment's thought, 'it's a deal.'

'It's a deal about what?' Beth asked. 'Telling about our first experiences or going for a job?'

'Both,' said Celeste. 'The job interview, if you insist. But I really meant about telling about our first time. Oh, what fun.'

She snuggled down into the bed, pulling Beth with her. Beth lay on her back, with Celeste's head on her shoulder. As Beth spoke, Celeste would occasionally nuzzle or lick the pink nipple just inches from her mouth. With her hand she idly played with Beth's pubic hair, twisting the silky curls around one finger.

'It was at school,' Beth said. 'I went to a private school in the Scottish lowlands, a girls only boarding school. I was just seventeen, and I was naïve and sexually innocent. It was a good school. I liked it there a lot.

'Anyway, we had all the normal games in the afternoons. You know the sort of thing – hockey in the winter, rounders or netball in the summer. In our house – my house was called Guilders – was a communal changing room, showers at one end, rows of pegs for hanging clothes and footlockers for shoes. It was the girls' own room in a way, the teachers never bothered to go in. I suppose it was too much of a mess.

'One whole corner of the changing room was another room, a sort of room within a room. It was the drying room, where we were supposed to hang our wet clothes. It had no windows, warm pipes around the walls so that it was always lovely and cosy and only one dim light. I don't suppose it was designed as a room to linger in, but we loved it, especially on cold days. It was like a sauna in a way, with benches along each wall.

'A group of girls would grab the drying room and defend it like a fort, repelling all boarders. You can imagine the sort of games. I was a popular girl, I think. I used to be let in to the drying room by the senior girls and sometimes we would stay there for hours.

'As the girls were dressing or undressing we would flick each other with wet towels. You know how much that hurts. One day a girl called Flo flicked one of the older girls and really hurt her. The older girl was angry, very angry. She grabbed Flo, who was wearing only her vest at the time, and smacked her bottom very hard. Suddenly we were all smacking her, taking it in turns to smack her bottom. I think Flo wanted to cry but we were all laughing so much I don't think she dared.

'Anyway, that became our regular game. Each day a group of girls would pick on just one for some imagined offence, like missing an open goal in hockey, and we would all gather round taking it in turns to smack her. We were quite democratic. Everyone was the victim at least once, but over a period of time it became mostly the less senior girls who were smacked and the older girls who did the smacking. They would always stop if a girl called out or worse, started crying. In a strange way we knew what we were doing was somehow wrong, and that's why it never went too far.

'When I was first smacked I quite enjoyed being the centre of attention, and I got the reputation of being a good sport. Any girl who was really upset could have told a teacher but no one ever did. Over a period of time, I found I was chosen more and more frequently. I was quite proud. Older girls seldom paid any attention at all to their juniors, but being an uncomplaining victim seemed to make me part of the gang.

'I came to see it as a matter of endurance, seeing how long I could go without calling for mercy. I remember I got up to seventy smacks one afternoon. It was a record at the time. I was probably sore that evening but there wasn't a prouder girl in the house. Silly, isn't it?

'Anyway, one particular afternoon I was the victim again. Imagine it; there I was, lying on my tummy on a towel on the floor, stark naked. Five or six girls were kneeling in a ring around me, taking it in turns to smack my bottom like a drum and counting as they did so. Suddenly the counting, and the smacking, stopped. I turned my head to see why, and there in the doorway was a prefect, a girl of about eighteen, a quiet girl called Jane Morrow.

'There was no big row, but the other girls, I remember, were confined to the school for two weeks and had extra detention. In the middle of prep that evening, I was called out and asked to go and see Jane Morrow in her study at the top of the house – prefects had their own studies. By and large they ran the school when the teachers weren't around.

'I don't remember much about Jane Morrow. She was quiet and played the violin very well, but she wasn't the sort of older girl I had a pash on. Those were the girls who had long legs and were good at games. They played the boys in school plays. Jane asked me what had been happening, and in my innocent way I explained the game and even told her about me trying for a record.

'She said the game would not be happening any more but said that there was no reason why I should still not try for the record – with her. And do you know, it didn't seem funny or odd to me. She made me take off my knickers and put me over her knee. I do remember thinking it odd that I didn't lie over her whole lap but that she put me between her legs, with my tummy on one thigh and my legs trapped from above by her other thigh.

'Then she smacked my bottom. It was thirty smacks that first time, I think. She pretended it was all a game and announced that it would be forty smacks the next time. I didn't understand then – but I do now – why her cheeks were so red and she looked so hot and bothered. I thought she was tired from her efforts.

'Our game went on about once a week for the rest of that term and until the end of the following term, before she left school. The last time I went to see her it was eight o'clock one evening. She had told me to be there then, but she pretended she had forgotten. She was just out of the shower and I could see she was naked under her bathrobe.

'She put me over her lap in the normal way with my legs between hers. My left thigh was right up against her groin, and I could feel her pubic hair. She started to spank me, but it was not like in the past. It was somehow wilder. She counted up to ten and then stopped counting. She was gasping and each time she smacked me she would push herself against me, rubbing against my leg. It went on and on, with her smacking and gasping and rubbing faster and faster. Suddenly, when the frenzy was at its height, she squealed and stopped. I felt used, as if I had done something wrong, but I was excited too. Strange things were happening in the pit of my stomach that had never surfaced before.

'Then she left and I grew up. Funny how I'd forgotten all that until yesterday when I was over Dr Susskind's knee.'

Celeste kissed Beth's nipple again. 'How sweet you must have been.'

Beth turned onto her side. 'Now it's your turn,' she said, snuggling in to the other girl. With one hand she stroked the bare, slightly stubbly patch where Celeste's pubic hair had been and idly squeezed together the lips of her sex.

'Must I?' Celeste pouted. 'That feels so good.'

Beth eased her fingers away. 'Yes, you must,' she said with mock severity.

Celeste reached for her hand and put it back where it had been. 'Oh, all right,' she said. 'My story is not so sweet. It was not so long ago and I was slightly older than you were. It was my first proper sexual experience. It was humiliating, disgusting and… very, very exciting. I still think about it now, when I am alone, if you know what I mean.'

Beth fingered Celeste's clitoris. 'You don't need to be alone now,' she purred.

Celeste opened her legs wider. 'Mmm, don't stop,' she said. 'Anyway, I went to France as an *au pair*. It was a summer job, to improve my French. We did not know the family beforehand but my father and the other man both worked for the same company, so everyone assumed I would be safe and well looked after.

'They were quite a wealthy family with a big house outside Chartres. I think the wife, Colette, had money of her own. I liked them all. There was Colette, her husband, Alain, and two children, a boy of five and a girl of three. They treated me well and I had a good time. I like everything about the French.

'Alain was certainly arrogant but charming with it. He was about forty-five and very good-looking. He was away a lot and I spent most of my time with Colette and the kids. I was a sort of half-child, half-adult depending on whom I was with.

'My duties were not arduous but I did have to bath the children in the evening and put them to bed. By then Colette would be tired of them and was probably getting ready to go out. They were very sociable.

'After I had been there for two weeks, Colette went to Paris for a long weekend. Her favourite aunt lived there, probably the one with the money. Alain was around, but he was mad about polo and golf and I was largely in charge on my own. That first day I was due to go out in the evening, with another English girl I had met. We were going to try a local disco, and Alain had promised to be back early.

'The kids had been awkward and difficult all day. I think they missed their mother; she was not often away overnight. At bath time they were a real pain. They were all sorts of trouble and the final straw came when Maurice, the boy, was getting out of the bath. Quite spitefully he scooped up handfuls of soapy water and threw them all over me. I was all dressed up ready to go out, wearing my one sexy dress and with my hair done. I was soaked, a real mess.

'Well, I flipped. I pulled Maurice out of the bath and slapped him hard, twice. He howled, and because he was crying because of what I'd done, Saskia, the little one, started crying too.

'I was screaming at them in broken French, and they were both bawling. Just at the height of it I looked up and Alain was standing in the doorway, with a face like thunder. He had come in, heard the noise and come immediately upstairs.

'He sent me off to change, quieted the children, gave them supper and put them to bed himself. He wouldn't let me help. When my friend came to pick me up he answered the door and told her that I would not be going out. He apologised and she went away; I heard it all from upstairs.

'Then he called me down to the sitting room. His English

86

was better than my French. He told me to pack my bags, and that I would be leaving the next day. I protested, I got angry, I even cried, but he was inflexible. He accused me of hitting Maurice and, stupidly, I denied it. He said he could see the marks on the boy's body. He wasn't having his children hit by strangers. I would have to go.

'I started pleading. I didn't want to go. I liked it there. I was enjoying myself. I could not go home for a boring summer with my parents. I had nowhere else to go. I had no money. I told him I would never do it again, if he relented. It had been a spur of the moment thing, but he wouldn't give in.

'Finally, he seemed to think it over and then announced that if I was staying I would not go unpunished. He would treat me in the same way I had treated Maurice, but with the greater severity appropriate for an adult. I should go away and think about it until bedtime. I should then either pack my bags ready to leave early the next morning, or I should report to him in the sitting room wearing my nightclothes.

'I went to my room to think it over but, to be honest, my mind was already made up; I was not going home. So I spent most of the two hours wondering what Alain would do.

'At eleven o'clock I went back downstairs. I was wearing a nightdress and dressing gown, but had bare feet. I had put on a little make-up and done my hair in a pretty way. If he had been waiting for me, he did not show it. He didn't even look surprised. He told me what he was going to do, and then it would be forgotten. There would be no arguments. He was going to spank me, as I had spanked Maurice. I protested at once that I had only smacked him twice, hardly a spanking, but he said that twice to a boy of his age was severe enough and that anyway, I had the choice; I could leave. Maurice had had no such choice.

'I stood my ground so he told me what to do. Maurice had been naked so I would be naked too. I had hit Maurice on the bottom so it would be my bottom that suffered. I had hit Maurice with my hand, but hands were inappropriate for me. I was shocked to then see him produce a bamboo cane. Lord knows where it came from.

'He told me to strip, so I did so, taking my robe and nightdress off very slowly. Silly me, I thought he would be overcome by my beauty and let me off. I stood in front of him stark naked, with my hands to my sides, not trying to hide anything. He looked me up and down carefully and made me turn around, but his eyes were cold. There might have been a passion there, in fact there was a passion there, but it was well hidden.

'He made me bend over the back of the sofa so that my head and arms were on the cushions on the other side. I can't imagine what I looked like, with just my legs and my bottom on show. He fiddled with the cane between my thighs, tapping from side to side, opening them up a little. I felt very embarrassed, as you can imagine. I had never been naked in front of a man before, and here I was showing Alain my most intimate bits in the most brazen way. But it was undeniably exciting.

'When I was in the required position I heard him cutting the cane through the air, and then he spoke. "I am going to give you six strokes, Claudine," he said. "And it is going to hurt."

'Claudine? Who was Claudine? Here I was, little Celeste, offering him my all and he was talking to Claudine. I found out later that Claudine was his secretary. Apparently

Claudine looked a little like me. Apparently she came from a very good family and was very haughty, but lazy and inefficient. She infuriated Alain but he could not do anything about her because he needed her family contacts for his business.

'But you can imagine how I felt. It was so humiliating. Here he was, wanting to chastise his secretary, who probably really deserved it, except it was my body he was using.

'He gave me six strokes as promised. It hurt like hell but I took it as well as I could. I was crying by the end, though. I must have looked awful, tear-stained cheeks, hair all mussed up. Then he was so sweet to me. He took me in his arms and comforted me. He kissed my tears and told me I had been brave, and before I knew it I was kissing him properly – real, deep, intense kisses. At that moment I loved him passionately, probably all the more so because of what he had just done to me.

'I begged him to make love to me. I wanted him to lay me down on the sofa and take me. And he would have done, but he astutely guessed that I was a virgin. He wouldn't do it the normal way after that, even though I begged him. He said he would have me all the same, he wanted me, but he would do it his way, so as to preserve my virginity. I remember I was disappointed, but I didn't care so long as he did something.

'He went and fetched a pot of lubricant. He made me rub it on my bottom and then over his cock. It was so beautiful – I wanted to suck it. Then he made me bend again over the back of the sofa, in the same position I had been for my caning… and you can guess what happened next. He sank his cock into my bottom. He was as gentle as he could be, but it hurt at first. Then it was wonderful;

the feeling of being utterly taken, of being totally debased.

'When it was over he put me to bed, and the next morning he licked me awake. It was wonderful. He taught me to do the same to him. We did that on and off for the next two months, as long as I stayed there. He never did it in my bottom again and he never fucked me, but oh, I wish he had.'

Beth lifted herself onto one elbow. 'I wonder if he ever caned Claudine in the end,' she mused.

Celeste stretched. 'I'd be jealous if he did. She would probably adore it, because he was a wonderful lover. Just thinking about him makes me feel sexy.'

Beth threw back the bedclothes and moved down the bed until she was lying between Celeste's legs. 'What's it like, being fucked in the bottom?' she asked bluntly.

Celeste was surprised. 'Have you never done it? It hurts at first, but it's very exciting.'

'Mmm,' Beth purred. 'Tell me about it all again, but this time tell me exactly what Alain did, and how he did it. You can imagine that I'm him.'

'Well...' Celeste sighed, 'start by putting one finger in my bottom...'

Chapter Seven

'Do you want this job or not?' Beth asked, with a note of asperity in her voice.

'Not much,' Celeste mumbled, holding a coffee cup to her lips.

Three days had passed since Beth first raised the matter of a job for Celeste at Rybix, and not once in the discussions since had the younger girl shown much interest. Now they were in a café around the corner from the Rybix building, their appointment with Kearns was just seventeen minutes away, and Beth was losing patience.

'Okay then,' Beth said, 'pay me the rent you owe me. Pay me for all the food you have eaten, the white wine you have drunk. Fend for yourself and see if you like it. If you won't make the effort, won't even try, I'm finished with you.'

Celeste took Beth's hand. 'Don't be angry with me,' she sulked. 'I'm scared – scared stiff. What's he like?'

'Father Christmas in a suit of armour. Tough as nails and sharp as a whip. But don't worry, he'll like you; you're just his type.'

'A what type is that?' Celeste asked.

'Cheeky but bright. You won't have to act, just be yourself.' She squeezed Celeste's fingers. 'Just give it a go. You have nothing to lose.'

'Except perhaps my modesty,' Celeste said dryly. Even though it was mid-summer, she was shivering very slightly.

'He may take to you immediately, just by looking at

you.' Celeste looked doubtful so Beth continued to reassure her. 'Do it for me, then. Do it for the rent. Do it to help me in my job. Do it for our relationship. And do it for your own bloody good, too.'

Celeste stood, suddenly looking determined, scraping her chair on the tiled floor. 'Okay, let's do it,' she said firmly. 'How do I look?'

An hour before Beth had helped Celeste to dress, choosing for her a short navy-blue skirt and a powder blue V-necked jumper, with a scarf tied loosely at the neck. 'Simple, elegant, and utterly desirable,' she said.

Kearns was in an expansive mood. He leant back in his chair with his thumbs hooked into his waistcoat pockets and a cigar smouldering in an ashtray on the desk in front of him.

'I know you are a friend of Beth, Ms Englund, and that is a recommendation in itself – I should know. But what would you bring to a job here?' he asked. 'Have you brought a curriculum vitae?'

'I, um, don't actually have a CV,' she said. 'I am my own CV. What you see is what you get.'

Kearns frowned a little. Beth, sitting in a chair alongside Celeste, quickly intervened. 'She's too young to have much history, T.J., but she has an aptitude for public relations and dealing with the media.'

Celeste stole a quick glance at Beth, with one eyebrow raised quizzically.

'If it is the case that what I see is what I get, would you mind standing up, so that I can look at you properly,' Kearns said. Celeste uncrossed her legs and stood facing him.

'First impressions are very important in public relations,'

he said. 'Now turn around.'

Celeste obediently turned so that her back was to Kearns.

'You certainly look the part,' Kearns decided, as Celeste resumed her seat. 'That's half the battle won, but what about the other half? Clients can be difficult. You would have a lot to learn.'

Beth spoke up again. 'I'm sure, T.J., that she could learn with your guidance. She is most certainly bright enough—'

'Let her speak for herself,' Kearns interrupted Beth.

'I could learn with your guidance, sir,' Celeste said, almost echoing her friend. 'If you helped me you would find that… that I learn very quickly.'

Beth could see that Celeste was struggling, so she took the risk of interjecting again. 'She sometimes lacks motivation and self-discipline, though. She needs a firm hand, and you, T.J., would be an ideal teacher.'

'A teacher, yes.' Kearns seemed to like the thought. 'I believe in encouraging young talent. Don't I, Beth? A kind word here, a rebuke there.'

Beth turned to Celeste, urging her with her eyes to wipe the doubtful look off her face. 'Mr Kearns can be very firm. Fair but firm. You would have to behave yourself.'

Celeste spoke, as if replying to Beth but looking at Kearns. 'Sometimes,' she said hesitantly, 'I do seem to get into trouble when I shouldn't.'

Kearns was silent for a moment, apparently lost in thought. 'What exactly are you proposing?' He looked at them both in turn. 'And I am not certain who that question should be addressed to,' he added with a slight smile.

'A three month contract,' Celeste said frankly.

'For a start,' Beth quickly intervened.

'As a personal assistant,' Celeste proposed.

'And public relations adviser,' Beth added.

'Weekends off, but no holidays.'

'I should hope not,' Kearns said. Again he appeared to be thinking. 'Mrs Woods is my general factotum and has been for years. We must not put her nose out of joint.'

Both girls nodded their agreement, and Kearns looked at Celeste. 'On occasion you might have to work late,' he pointed out. 'And I travel a lot. There are times when I might want you with me, to deal with the press and clients and so on. Do you speak any languages?'

Celeste stole a sideways glance at Beth. 'I'm not bad at oral French,' she said, and Beth put a hand over her mouth to suppress a gasp. 'But I am not very good at writing it.'

Kearns picked up a pen and twiddled with it. 'We seem to be working towards a conclusion,' he said. 'Now there's the question of where I would put you.'

Beth spoke up. 'I was thinking of Mrs Woods' office outside. She could…' Her voice tailed off as Kearns shook his head.

'That wouldn't do at all,' he said. He stood up and walked to the wall at one side of his desk. He raised a hand and beckoned to them to join him. As they watched, he pressed a button and the wooden panelling slid noiselessly to one side, revealing a short, narrow staircase leading downwards only.

'Welcome to my inner sanctum,' he said. 'Not even Mrs Woods knows when I leave the office and retreat down here.'

'Um, that looks like my cue to leave you two alone,' Beth said.

'No, I'd like you to stay,' Kearns said.

'Yes, please don't go,' Celeste added.

Kearns led the way down the short flight of carpeted

steps. 'It's a dungeon,' Celeste gasped, and made a gesture towards the main office door, silently suggesting to Beth that they beat a hasty retreat. But Beth took her firmly by the hand and pulled her after Kearns.

'This is where I stay when I'm in town,' he was saying conversationally. 'My family are in Oxfordshire and I can't always get home.' He opened a door and guided the girls into a small apartment, comfortable rather than luxurious. 'We're one floor down,' he said. 'Marketing and public relations are just through there.' He waved a hand airily in a vague direction.

He led the two girls into a hallway. 'And between them and me,' he said, opening another door, 'I just happen to have a spare office. Bare at the moment, but nice and handy.'

Celeste looked slightly glum at the lack of furniture.

'It could be lovely,' said Beth.

He took the girls back into his sitting room. 'Take a seat,' he said, and then looked at Beth, nodding towards a cabinet. 'Help yourself to a drink. Now we are alone and not in danger of being overheard, I think I should find out more about this young lady I am considering taking on.'

'Perhaps now I should go,' Beth said.

Celeste looked at her pleadingly, and Kearns said, 'No, stay – I insist.'

'Er, I'd like to know more about the contract, if I may,' Celeste piped up, and Beth glanced at her admiringly.

Kearns replied by picking up a telephone, apparently a direct line to Mrs Woods. 'I'm downstairs, Mary. I may be a little while. Draw up an employment contract for a Miss Celeste Englund. I'll give you the address later. Three months. Public relations adviser.' When he mentioned the fee, Celeste's eyes widened.

'That'll pay the rent,' Beth said quietly.

Kearns was still talking quite loudly, obviously wanting the girls to listen. 'Put in the standard get out clause, one week's trial. Either side can terminate.' He listened for a moment and then said in a normal tone, 'No, I haven't yet told Jim. But I will.' He listened again. 'No. No. I won't, I promise.' He laughed. 'Behave yourself. You remember too many things too well.'

He replaced the receiver with a smile on his lips. 'That should answer your questions,' he said to Celeste. 'Now, how about answering mine?'

'What would you like to know?' Celeste asked.

'The matter of ill discipline,' he said, taking a seat. 'What am I supposed to do when you let me down or misbehave?'

'But I won't,' Celeste insisted.

Kearns looked at Beth, and she spoke without looking at Celeste. 'I find a good spanking helps,' she said.

'I can see she could be the difficult type,' said Kearns. 'But a good spanking helps, you say? You would know, of course, as I remember only too well—'

'I'd rather not talk about that, thank you,' Beth interrupted him. 'But yes, a similar scenario to that. I find it works wonders with her.'

'Would you not talk about me when I'm right here,' Celeste protested.

Kearns ignored her. 'Has she been spanked recently, Beth?'

'Just the other day,' she confirmed. 'She asked for and received a real thrashing.'

'And this thrashing, Beth,' Kearns went on, 'was it on her bare bottom?'

'Oh yes, T.J. It would not have been half as effective if it were not.'

'Why don't you ask me?' Celeste complained. 'I can speak, you know.'

Kearns looked at her calmly. 'Was it on your bare bottom, my dear?'

'It might have been,' Celeste said sulkily, shrugging her shoulders.

'And was it effective?'

Celeste shrugged again. 'How would I know?'

Kearns looked at Beth. 'If it was effective, the effect didn't last long, it seems. I think perhaps we – you – should try again. Now.'

'Me?' asked Beth.

'Yes, you,' said Kearns. 'You brought her here, you introduced her to me, you told me she can do the job. You are responsible.'

'But T.J., I thought you would do it, if anyone,' Beth said. 'I don't want to spank her here, in front of you.'

Kearns' voice was grave. 'Don't make me remind you, Beth, that we have only just signed a contract with your firm. I could break it very easily now, before it comes into force, with only a very small default payment.'

'Oh, isn't this fun,' Celeste said sarcastically. 'The two of you discussing in front of me which of you is going to do the spanking. This is *me* you are talking about.'

'Shut up,' Beth snapped.

'You were right,' Kearns said, 'she can be very difficult. I suggest you show me the remedy now or we can call the whole thing off.'

'Stand up,' Beth almost barked at Celeste. She was surprised how angry she felt. She was angry with Kearns, but angrier still with Celeste. She was not going to let the girl ruin everything with her disrespectful ways.

'No, I won't,' Celeste refused adamantly, gripping the

arms of the chair.

Beth looked at Kearns; he gave her no clues, but turned to Celeste, speaking calmly and quietly. 'Young lady, before I buy an expensive present I am accustomed to having a good look at what I am getting for my money. If I am paying a small fortune for your services, I expect at least the same privilege.'

Beth stood alongside Celeste's chair. 'Take off your skirt and knickers,' she ordered.

For a brief moment that felt like an eternity no one moved, and then Celeste stood up and turned her back on Kearns. 'You'll pay for this,' she murmured to Beth, reaching for her skirt.

'Everything off, I think,' said Kearns, putting his feet up on the coffee table.

'Do as you're told,' Beth said to Celeste. 'Take everything off.'

As Celeste began to undress, Beth felt her anger fade. Celeste had been awkward but that was understandable. Kearns had been just as she had expected but even more generous than she anticipated. She did not have to get undressed, at least not at the moment. It was just the two of them and a semi-naked Celeste. She was beginning to enjoy herself.

It was like being an announcer at a fashion show. She should give a running commentary on each new act. She might be ashamed of herself later on, and undoubtedly Celeste would be furious with her and seek revenge, but this was fun. She could become quite good at it, she thought. And anyway, Celeste could not really complain; she had asked her to stay.

'You'll see how lovely she is,' she said to the watching man. 'Lovely and wilful.'

Celeste had already taken off her scarf and pulled the jumper over her head. Now she was unhooking her bra, and as she threw it to one side, her breasts quivered invitingly.

'Aren't they lovely?' Beth said, cupping the nearest breast in one hand. 'So soft and so, so sensitive.' She pinched the nipple between her thumb and forefinger, and Celeste squealed.

'Take off the rest,' Beth instructed, and Celeste sullenly kicked off her shoes and unhooked her skirt, which fell to the floor.

'And the best is yet to come,' Beth said, addressing Kearns again.

Slowly, facing him, Celeste pushed her panties down her thighs, past her knees and kicked them to one side.

'Look T.J.,' Beth said. 'An unobstructed view. No pubic hair. Isn't she sensational?' She spoke to Celeste. 'Open your legs. No false modesty. Let T.J. see you clearly.' With flashing eyes Celeste obeyed. Kearns said nothing, but stared directly at the naked beauty standing before him.

'So lovely,' Beth said. 'And so inviting.' She ran her forefinger up over the exposed lips. She licked her finger and then replaced it, holding the soft labia open. 'Good enough to eat.

'And now, the *pièce de résistance*,' she went on, and turned Celeste around. 'Just look at that,' she said, but found her words were unnecessary. Kearns was already staring at Celeste's bottom. 'Isn't it absolutely flawless?' Beth said. 'Made for love and punishment.'

She cupped one buttock in her hand, feeling its weight. 'Excellent skin tone, fine tensile strength and,' she said, 'superb musculature control. If you could bottle it you would make a fortune! T.J., you're a very lucky man.'

She placed her hand against the small of Celeste's back, making her bend forward. 'A beautiful bottom, but a naughty one,' she went on. 'Touch your toes.'

When Celeste was bent double and the skin of her bottom was as taut as a drum, Beth spanked it once, hard across both cheeks. Her small hand left a red mark on either side of the cleft.

'A bottom to be spanked – hard and often,' she said, and again she struck, this time on only one cheek.

'A bottom to be paddled.' She spanked her again on the other cheek.

'A bottom to be slippered.' She spank her again.

'A bottom to be caned.' Yet another.

'A bottom to be whipped.' And yet another.

She then stroked Celeste, fondling both buttocks and rubbing away the hurt. 'Personally,' she said, 'I prefer the hand. I like to feel my palm against her pliable flesh.'

She looked at Kearns. 'She has been caned, you know. Not so very long ago.'

She smacked Celeste again. 'You were caned, weren't you?'

'Yes,' Celeste croaked.

'How many strokes?'

'Six.'

'And what did he do when he finished caning you?'

'He – he screwed me.'

'Where?'

Celeste said nothing.

'Where did he screw you?' Beth persisted, spanking her again.

'I-in my bottom,' Celeste whispered.

'Say it again; I don't think T.J. could hear you.'

'In my bottom,' she said louder. 'He screwed me in my bottom.'

Beth spanked her again. 'Open your legs wider.' Celeste moved her feet. 'Now hold open your cheeks.'

Celeste raised her hands and pulled her buttocks apart.

'You see, T.J?' Beth gloated triumphantly. 'He screwed her in this delectable little opening.' She placed her index finger on the vulnerable little anus. 'You wouldn't believe it, would you? You wouldn't believe something so small and beautiful could accommodate an erect penis. Of course, yours is exceptional, if I may say so. I am not so certain yours could be accommodated here.'

Kearns' hands moved to his trousers, and she watched him unzip them and his fingers disappear inside.

She went on talking. 'You'll find, T.J., when you know her better, just how naughty Celeste can be.' She smacked the younger girl's glorious bottom again, making her gasp and sway slightly.

Kearns had pulled out his cock and was stroking it gently, running a finger up and down the underside. It was as wide and as impressive as Beth remembered, and as rigid as a board.

'The naughty little tart plays with herself, too,' Beth said, appearing to pay no attention to Kearns. 'I've caught her at it.'

'No, I don't,' Celeste objected pitifully.

'Oh, yes you do,' Beth insisted, smacking her again. 'Like you are just about to, aren't you?'

Celeste said nothing, so Beth smacked her hard several more times.

'Aren't you?' she repeated.

Still Celeste said nothing, but the fingers of her right hand appeared between her legs, obscuring her labia.

Kearns got out of his seat and moved forward until he was only a couple of feet from the two lovely girls. He was stroking his penis fully now, his hand moving up and down the shaft. The unseeing eye at its head pointed directly at Celeste's anus, as her forefinger disappeared between her moist lips. With her other hand she rubbed her clitoris, moaning slightly, and her bottom began to sway and her buttocks clench, encouraged by the smarting smacks delivered by Beth.

Beth knew the time had come for her to stop talking and to get spanking again. She took her beat from the movement of the man's hand, smacking Celeste hard on each stroke. As the bottom in front of her turned a deep red, she could hear Celeste's moans turn into panting pleasure, and she knew her friend well enough to know she was just about to come.

Kearns' fist was pumping with increasing vigour, Beth's hand was furiously smacking the proffered bottom, and Celeste's fingers were working avidly between her trembling thighs. The three moved independently but together, and just as Beth thought she could strike no faster, Kearns gave a strangled groan and a cascade of semen shot through the air in an arc and landed on Celeste's bottom, at the top of the shadowy valley. It began to trickle down towards her tiny anus as she wailed and her hips convulsed, her buttocks tensing and wetness shining like silver on her fingers. Beth stopped spanking her, but the grimacing man's second ejaculation occurred, albeit with less momentum, and fell warmly over her hand.

'I don't believe you did that,' Celeste said ten minutes later as the two girls walked down the street away from the Rybix building.

'Neither do I,' Beth confided, and then they had gone three or four more paces when she added, 'What do you mean, you don't believe I did that? I don't believe *you* did that.'

'Well, I don't believe either of us did that,' Celeste said, as they entered the same café as before.

They were giggling with relief as they ordered some coffee, like schoolgirls let out at the end of a long, hard exam.

'You are a very, very naughty girl who should be ashamed of herself,' Beth said fondly, then let out a little whoop of delight. 'But it worked. He's hiring you.'

'And you,' Celeste said with mock severity, 'are a witch. I never knew you were like that.'

'I'm not really,' Beth replied. 'I don't know what came over me.' She pretended to look glum, and then a mischievous smile lit up her face. 'But let's go home and do it again.'

'Yes, let's,' Celeste enthused. 'Only this time we'll change places. You owe me.'

Chapter Eight

It was mid-morning, but in the studio the sun was setting. The back projection screen at one end of the airy room was a glorious dusky red. In front of the screen was a trellis covered in bougainvillaea, two small palm trees and a flowering hibiscus, a table and chairs of wrought iron painted white, and three girls in beachwear, shivering with cold.

The photographer, Peter Parnell, was walking around the room, pulling down blinds and switching on lights. 'For goodness' sake, get them a blow heater,' he snapped at a pimply youth with long hair who was trying to look busy and interested in a light meter, as he cast covert glances at the breasts of a redhead in a bikini.

At the other end of the room, Beth sat in a chair with her arms folded and a clipboard and folder on her lap. She was present to supervise the shoot and she deliberately arrived early. As the Cross, Carstairs and Denton account manager for Rybix, this was her first big job for the company, a poster campaign promoting Rybix ice cream. She had made sure to hire Parnell, known to be irritable but a good photographer, and to choose the best looking models. Now it was up to them; there was not much she could do at this point while they were setting up.

She was glad of the momentary respite as she had a lot on her mind. Richard Cross, for one. She caught herself thinking about him often these days. But what exactly did she want from him?

An affair? Maybe.

To finish the unfinished business? That was more like it.

She could admit it to herself; she wanted Richard to make love to her properly, to respect her, if only for a short while. She wanted to prove to herself that she had power over him. So what had gone wrong? Why had nothing developed since that day she was naked on her knees in front of him and his wife walked in on them? Two weeks had gone by without any further moves from him, without any real contact at all. Two weeks of the month had already gone by and she'd hardly seen him since that day.

It cannot have been because of his wife, she thought. Both Richard and Helen acted as if they enjoyed every second of it – or at least as if they were in agreement. He had been busy since then, she knew, but it was more than that. The thought struck her that maybe it was the Rybix account she successfully secured for the company. Maybe that was it. What a quandary. Maybe he only fancied her when he wanted to punish her. And how could he punish her when she had just brought in an enormous new account? Could that be possible? Her success could be her own undoing. Stupid man; he could punish her any time he liked, she thought, imagining being across his lap again. She must discuss it with Dr Susskind at their next appointment.

'Beth,' a voice called, and she looked up to find Parnell in front of her. 'I'm ready,' he said, 'but aren't there supposed to be four girls?'

'Of course,' Beth replied, rifling through the papers on her lap. 'Who's missing?' She looked at the set-up. The three girls, warmer now but bored, were acting up on behalf of the pimply youth looking at them through a camera viewfinder. As Beth watched they turned in a line away from him, bent down and pushed down the bottom halves of their bikinis, revealing three bottoms as pink as the sunset behind them. Then they collapsed into each other's arms, howling with laughter as the young man emerged from behind the camera looking all flustered.

'Oh, a new girl, Natasha Perry,' she said.

'Well she's late,' Parnell snapped impatiently. 'She should be sacked before she starts.'

'She should be smacked,' Beth corrected, under her breath.

'Did someone mention my name?' asked a breathless voice from behind them. A small dark girl stood by the door, her cheeks pink as if she had been running.

Having chosen her from a composite Beth was glad to see the model in the flesh, and she liked what she saw. Natasha was cute and petit, and she would make a pleasing contrast to the comfortably endowed girls already present. And she was certainly *very* pretty.

'Get out of your street clothes and into a swimsuit,' Parnell told her, pointing to a side door that led to a dressing room. 'As quickly as you can.'

Five minutes later he was in his element, directing the four girls, a make-up artist and his assistant, as if he was staging a major production. 'You're on the veranda of a grand house on a beautiful Caribbean island at the end of a perfect day,' he said. 'You are the cool people, the jet set, enjoying what the cool people enjoy; ice cream.'

As the assistant placed tall glasses containing a pink concoction on the wrought iron table, Parnell went on. 'Don't eat it, just pretend; it's really mashed potatoes. Cold, pink mashed potatoes. Real ice cream melts.'

Beth watched as Parnell positioned the girls and redirected the lights. The assistant turned on a fan, so that a breeze ruffled the girls' hair.

'There,' Parnell said finally. 'The coolest way to end the day.'

They'd have to work on that slogan, Beth thought, as the shooting began. She admired Parnell's uncharacteristic patience and his professionalism whilst shooting. She could see why he was amongst the best in the business; the pains he took to get everything, each strand of hair, each delicate flower, just right. Even the plain and dowdy looked their best in a Parnell picture, and the attractive looked utterly gorgeous.

The models were aware of his reputation. When the Rybix shoot was over they crowded around him, asking that he take portrait shots of them for their portfolios. He reluctantly agreed and although he shot the photographs quickly, he still took great care to do as good a job as he could within a short time. When they had left for the dressing room, talking excitedly amongst themselves, Parnell turned to Beth with a questioning look.

'It looked good,' she said. 'I can't wait to see the results.'

Parnell studied her face closely. 'You know, you're prettier than that lot. I should photograph you, for your album.'

He turned away, dispatching his assistant to the dark room, and began to clear up the 'veranda'. Beth followed him to help.

'You really think so?' she asked, picking up the potted hibiscus, the germ of an idea forming in her head.

Parnell looked at her face again, now framed by white, scented flowers. 'Sure,' he said. 'I've got more than an hour left, and you're paying for my time anyway.'

'Well, okay, but we'd better wait until the other girls have gone,' she said excitedly, carrying the plant to the door.

Fifteen minutes later the girls had gone and the pimply assistant, Joe, had been sent to lunch.

'Let's get you into a good light,' Parnell said. 'Soft and honey-coloured like your hair.' He fiddled around for ages, changing the lights and filters, shooting off test pictures, seeming to take far more care with Beth than he had with the portraits of the girls.

And Beth was flattered. 'You don't have to try so hard, you know,' she said. 'We'll still be coming back to you for more work.'

Parnell laughed her remark off. 'But you're worth it,' he said. 'You really are very lovely, and natural. I am trying to capture that.'

When finally he was happy with every detail, he shot off two complete films of her head and shoulders, muttering instructions every now and then. Eventually he told her to relax. 'That should do,' he said. 'One or two of them looked really good.'

'Do… do you ever shoot nudes?' Beth ventured to ask, trying to appear casual, and instead of replying directly he beckoned her to a bookcase and selected a large green folder. Beth leafed through it. On each page was a different nude; men and women, very sexy but not obscene. Many of the subjects gleamed with oil and looked as if they had been burnished like polished brass. Beth was impressed. They were good enough for a gallery, especially the ones of the men. The men looked as if they had been photographed with love; the women with admiration.

Beth did not look at him. 'Would, um, would you shoot me like that, in the nude, Peter?' she asked, adding, 'It would be for a friend – a very close friend.'

'Those take hours,' he said, nodding at the folder in her hands, but when she looked crestfallen he relented. 'But I suppose we could do one or two, just to see how they look. Ah well, there goes my lunch.'

He waved her to the dressing room. 'There should be a robe behind the door,' he told her.

As she was undressing, Beth remembered with delight that the diamond pendant was in her bag. She intended to take it to the jewellers that afternoon to be cleaned. When she was naked, she fastened it around her neck and admired herself in the full length mirror. Then, putting on the robe, it suddenly struck her how strange the situation was; a situation she had created. She was not worried about Parnell seeing her naked; he was a professional photographer and anyway, she had heard that he was gay. But she had also heard that he was an outrageous gossip, and that did suddenly worry her. She certainly did not want this, her taking advantage of a perk of her job, to backfire.

When she reappeared in the studio Parnell was bent behind the camera at the same set-up he had used for the portraits. Beth moved straight to her spot, dropped the robe and started posing, thrusting her full breasts towards the camera.

'Wow,' Parnell muttered, straightening up and looking directly at her chest. He approached and cupped the diamond pendant in his hand, admiring it closely. Beth could not help smiling, because he hadn't even noticed the perfect twin cushions between which the pendant rested. So the stories she'd heard about him must be right;

her natural female vanity certainly would not permit any other conclusion.

Parnell returned to the viewfinder and resumed his directions: Right arm up, demure not obvious, left knee bent, shake the hair loose.

After several clicks of the shutter Beth turned around. 'From behind as well, please Peter,' she purred.

A few more clicks later and she bent forward, almost double.

'I didn't tell you to move,' Parnell said.

'But I want some close-ups of my bottom.'

'And I can see why,' Parnell said admiringly. 'Let me guess – they're for the friend.'

There was another click and then the sound of the motor as the film rewound. As Parnell changed it, Beth plucked up her courage. 'Peter,' she said sweetly, 'I want my bottom to be reddened a little. You know, as if… as if… you know, as if I've been spanked for being naughty.'

Parnell looked up from the camera in his hands, his expression frozen for a moment. 'Oh, he's like that is he, your friend? I assume it is a he. Likes naughty girls, does he?' He looked back at the camera and added quietly, 'They're not the sort of photographs I usually take. I have a reputation to think about, you know.'

'You have, Peter,' Beth agreed. 'A very good one, if not the best. But just this once – for me? No one will ever know.'

As he fitted the camera back on the tripod, Beth resumed her position, bending down away from the lens. Parnell approached her. 'A little shade of red might be aesthetically pleasing, I suppose,' he said, without much enthusiasm, and he lightly slapped her bottom.

Beth sighed impatiently. 'Harder, Peter,' she urged.

'Harder. It has to be red—'

'Excuse me,' someone said from the other end of the room. 'I don't mean to interrupt.'

Beth straightened up quickly, wheeling around and reaching for her robe at the same time. 'Who let you in?' she gasped, unable to see the figure clearly because of the lights in her eyes. 'Who are you?'

'You should learn to knock,' Parnell said angrily, moving away from Beth.

'I'm sorry,' said the figure, approaching into the light. 'It's only me – Natasha Perry. I think I left my bag behind.' She spoke in a breathless rush. 'Luckily we were having lunch in a pub just around the corner when I realised.

'Don't mind me, though,' the lovely girl added, and darted to the dressing room, returning a moment later carrying a large cloth bag. 'Got it,' she said brightly, but made no attempt to leave.

'We are rather busy,' Beth said, trying to appear unflustered.

'So I see,' Natasha smirked cheekily. 'I couldn't help noticing when I came in.' Beth was annoyed to see the slight smile playing around the girl's lips. Her eyes were sparkling and her cheeks were still flushed.

Natasha turned to Parnell. 'May I stay and watch?' she asked. 'It looked like an interesting shoot.'

'No, you may not,' Beth retorted for him, grasped the girl by the arm and led her towards the exit. 'This is not the way to get future work, you know,' she said, almost pushing Natasha through the door.

'I'm sorry,' she said. 'I didn't mean to intrude. It's just that you're so attractive I couldn't help looking. I hope I see you again some time.'

After she had gone, Beth knew she would have to start

all over again to persuade Parnell to take the photographs she wanted. He protested that the spell was broken and that time was short. In return, she pleaded that it would only take a matter of minutes, but he would not budge and began to pack away some of his equipment.

They were still debating the situation when there was a knock on the door. 'That bloody girl,' Beth snapped, striding across the room. 'What now?' she barked as she flung open the door.

It wasn't Natasha, but Celeste, and with a straight face she announced, 'I am from marketing and media at Rybix. I've come to see how everything is going.'

'Who is this young man?' Parnell said, approaching behind Beth.

The words of introduction stuck in Beth's throat. Young man? Celeste, a young man? She looked closely at her friend, who playfully winked at her. She could be a young man, Beth thought. She looked at her friend's slender figure, her short hair, strong eyebrows, dark trouser suit, white shirt, tie, and little make-up. She could indeed be a young man.

'This is, um, Charlie,' Beth said to Parnell, choosing the first name that came into her head. 'Sh… he's a friend of mine. He works for Rybix.'

'Not the friend in question, I hope,' Parnell said to Beth, his eyes glued to Celeste. 'I'm Peter Parnell,' he said to her. 'Welcome to my den, Charlie.'

'No, not the friend in question,' Beth told him. 'But a good friend, all the same.'

Parnell took Celeste by the arm. 'You might be just what we are looking for, Charlie,' he said, unable to hide his attraction for what he thought was a slightly effeminate male. 'An answer to this maiden's prayer, so to speak.'

He looked at Beth, and she realised he was interested again in her request – even excited by what might develop from it. So the brief impasse was settled.

'Why don't we use Charlie in your photographs?' he suggested.

'Use me, in what way?' Celeste asked, and Beth noted with amusement that she dropped her voice a little.

Parnell turned to Beth. 'I think you should explain it to Charlie,' he said.

So Beth did; about the photographs she wanted, and how she therefore needed a light spanking just for the colourful effect.

'Then why not use make-up?' Celeste said, and Beth knew her friend was being deliberately awkward.

'Because it wouldn't look right, it would show,' she said.

'So I get to spank you,' Celeste said with a smile. 'What, right now? Here and now?'

'No, over here, Charlie,' Parnell said. 'I'll use you in the shot.'

'Only in one or two,' Beth countered. 'I want some close-ups too.'

When the two girls were in front of the lights, Beth took off the robe again and bent down before her friend. As Parnell busied himself behind the camera, Celeste enjoyed her new role. 'What a beautiful bottom,' she said, to no one in particular. 'A magnificent target, don't you think?'

'Not quite yet,' said Parnell. 'I'm not ready.'

'Just there, I think,' Celeste said, running her hand over the middle of Beth's bottom, the most prominent part of the inviting cheeks.

'Okay,' said Parnell, 'I'm ready now.'

Celeste smacked Beth hard, shook her hand and then smacked her again. 'It's working,' she said. 'Your bottom is going quite a lovely shade of pink.' With that, she smacked her twice more.

All the while Parnell was shooting; the two girls could hear the click of the shutter.

'Can you see the marks?' Beth asked Parnell, her voice a little strained, betraying the stinging tingle she was feeling in her beaten buttocks.

'Yes,' he said, 'but maybe one or two more would really do the trick.'

Beth clutched her knees even tighter and Celeste delivered a flurry of smacks on the middle of the delicious target in front of her.

'You look really good, Charlie,' Parnell encouraged from behind his camera. 'Really quite masterful.'

'That does it,' Beth said, standing up. 'You two are enjoying this too much.'

'But it's for your benefit,' Parnell reminded her. 'This is all at your insistence.'

'Your bottom is quite scarlet now,' Celeste added. 'And I'm beginning to enjoy this.'

'Too bad,' Beth said, pushing her out of shot. 'Now,' she said to Parnell, 'some close-ups of my bottom, please. The marks do show, don't they?'

'They do,' Celeste confirmed, clearly proud of her handiwork, 'but I'll happily provide some more.'

When the shoot was over Beth put on the robe, and as she was heading for the dressing room she heard Celeste say, 'Photography's such an interesting profession, Peter. May I call you Peter? I'd love to see more of what you do,' and Beth almost choked on a laugh as she heard Parnell invite her friend to see his darkroom sometime.

'I'm going to stay behind for a while,' Celeste announced, once Beth was dressed again and re-emerged from the dressing room. 'Peter is going to show me how things here work.'

'Charlie can bring you the negatives of the Rybix ice cream shoot and the prints of the best of your shots later,' Parnell added. 'He can help me with some developing.'

Beth looked at Celeste. 'Bring with you all the negatives and all the prints, and contacts,' she said.

'Yes, ma'am,' Celeste replied, with a cheeky mock salute.

Beth was already at home by the time Celeste returned in the evening. Celeste threw her a large envelope. 'The photographs are good,' she said. 'You don't look bad, either.'

Beth leafed through the sheets inside. 'How was it?' she asked idly. 'How long did you stay?'

Celeste giggled. 'He thought we were lovers, you and me,' she told her.

'We are lovers,' Beth pointed out.

'Not that way, silly,' Celeste said. 'Boy and girl lovers.' She blushed slightly. 'But he did find out that we weren't.'

'And how, exactly, did he find out?' Beth demanded.

Celeste's blush deepened. 'How do you think?' she said impishly.

'You *didn't*.'

'I did,' Celeste said, looking smug.

'The poor man must have been shattered,' Beth said, immediately worrying about her professional relationship with Parnell. 'Finding out you're not a young man, and that he'd made a fool of himself. He wouldn't have liked that at all.'

'Oh, I don't know,' Celeste replied airily. 'I think he really enjoyed it all, in the end.'

'Enjoyed it all?' As the meaning of her friend's words sank in, a smile broke out on Beth's face. 'Do tell.'

'Shan't,' Celeste replied, but she too was smiling.

'Tell, or I'll spank it out of you.'

So Celeste took up the classic stance of a storyteller, standing with her back to the fireplace, hands behind her bottom, feet slightly apart. She began to rock gently on her heels. With her smart suit and short hair, Beth thought, she really did look like a handsome young male.

'It all began in the darkroom,' Celeste said, using her 'Charlie' voice. 'He seemed very keen to impress me; you know, how good he is at photography and how much he knows about it. He got me to do some of the work. I helped to develop the photographs of you. As you can guess it was very warm and dark in there, and quite cramped. Every time I was working at a bench I would find him pressed up against my back, his groin against my bum. He was guiding me but enjoying himself at the same time – I could feel it. When the prints of you were developing, he said what a nice bottom you had and asked me if it had turned me on, spanking you, and then he mentioned my bottom as well. There was nothing, he said, like a tight male bum compared to the female version. Bloody cheek of the man. I could see the way his mind was working. He told me how much he could help me in my career, what he would do for me, and all the time he was rubbing himself harder and harder against me.

'Well, guess what happened next!' she giggled, and then told her friend before she could even think of an answer. 'He came in his pants!'

'No!' Beth smirked.

Celeste nodded enthusiastically. 'Yes! And that was it for a while, as he had to get his breath back. So while he was waiting for the prints of the Rybix stuff, looking just a bit embarrassed with himself, he showed me some of his equipment.'

Beth smiled, and Celeste quickly retorted, 'No, not that, I mean his *camera* equipment. It must cost thousands. There was a darling miniature camera, with a remote control. I didn't even know they existed. It was so cute, I'm afraid it found its way into my pocket.'

'It did what?' Beth queried incredulously. 'I don't believe you, Celeste.'

'I was only borrowing it,' Celeste said plaintively. 'Anyway, he caught me. He found it on me. He was close to me again and he patted my hip. He felt it in my pocket. I said I just wanted to borrow it, but he didn't believe me. He said I would have to pay a price for being a thief. He started undoing my belt and I thought he was going to beat me with it. He turned me around, squashed me up against one of his workbenches, pulled my trousers and knickers down, pulled his own trousers down and stuffed his cock right between my buttocks! It was weird! He started to rub against me, and as he did so he slid his hands around to my front, but when he found what was and what wasn't there, you can imagine his reaction!'

Beth nodded, her mouth open and her eyes wide.

'He was furious,' Celeste went on. 'He accused me of trying to make a fool of him and said I would pay for it. No more gentleness and understanding. He told me to lubricate his knob with my mouth. So I did. Then he made me lean right over the workbench again with my legs apart. He said that if I pretended to be a boy I would be treated like a boy. He then pressed his cock right into

117

me – right into my bottom. It hurt a little, but he loved it. And he lasted a very long time, probably because he'd messed his pants not so long before. He was gripping my hips and panting frantically, shunting back and forth, in and out of my poor bottom. He kept telling me that's what I could expect for trying to make a fool of him.

'Then when I was leaving, he told me I could borrow the camera whenever I wanted and that I already knew the price. He didn't seem angry by then. He told me I was an honorary young man. He didn't even want to know my real name. He would continue to call me Charlie.'

'You poor baby.' Beth stood up and put her arms around her young friend. 'You need a gentle touch now. I'll run you a bath.' As she was leaving the room, she said, 'Men are such brutes…' and then she giggled. 'But then of course you know that; you were one for a couple of hours!'

Chapter Nine

Beth took her time strolling to the jeweller's shop the next morning. It was a lovely day following an even nicer night – oh, what a night! She never realised that two girls and one vibrator could have such fun. After her bath and a good supper she had seduced 'Charlie' by performing a striptease and lap dancing until 'he' was overcome with lust. The vibrator held upright between 'his' legs was the evidence.

Celeste made Beth watch as she fitted the blunt end of the vibrator between her legs, lightly gripped by the lips of her vagina. 'This is my penis, girl – worship it,' she ordered, and Beth dutifully sank to her knees and took the still vibrator into her mouth, wetting its smooth surface.

'Oh,' Beth gasped, 'please use it on me.'

'I will,' Celeste retorted, 'and I want you on your hands and knees.'

Beth obediently fell onto all fours, her bottom in the air. With difficulty, Celeste held one end of the vibrator in place while the other penetrated Beth's sex. Shrieks of amusement had turned to moans of rapture as the electric penis worked its magic on both girls. It was a rapture heightened by watching themselves in the wall mirror, two pink and beautiful bodies connected by a pink and vibrating dildo.

Then it had been Beth's turn to be 'Charlie'…

No wonder she was warm now, she thought; it was not just due to the sun!

In the jeweller's she handed over the pendant to be cleaned. As the assistant was filling out the receipt Beth spotted a number of picture frames, exactly what she needed for Richard's present. She particularly liked an embossed silver frame, and taking the folder from her briefcase, surreptitiously slid out the full length nude photograph of her wearing the pendant, to make sure it would fit. And it was perfect – very expensive – but perfect. He would love it, so to hell with the cost.

Outside the shop she glanced at her watch and realised that she was really late for work, but even this did not ruffle her good humour; no one would mind, least of all Richard once he received his present.

About ten seconds after entering the office, however, her good humour evaporated. Something was wrong. A secretary looked at her with a cocked eyebrow.

'Where is everyone?' Beth asked.

'In the boardroom, where you are supposed to be,' the secretary replied. 'Richard has been looking for you,' she added with a note of malicious pleasure in her voice.

Without stopping to brush her hair or check her make-up, Beth rushed to the boardroom. She knocked and opened the door, and was appalled to see at least a dozen people inside, sitting around the long, polished table, listening intently to Richard Cross.

He looked up and frowned when he saw her, then turned to the others. 'I see Ms Forrester has arrived,' he said precisely. 'We have waited this long, perhaps you won't mind waiting a further minute or two.' He stood up and walked to the door, ushering her back outside with him.

'Where the hell have you been?' he demanded.

'Shopping,' Beth said lamely.

'Shopping?' The word came out with a sibilant hiss of

suppressed fury. '*Shopping?*' He was quivering, almost white with anger. 'They are the Internat crowd and you've been shopping!'

Beth slapped her forehead with the palm of one hand. 'Oh, shit!' she exclaimed. 'I completely forgot,' she added weakly.

'Forgot. You forgot.' His voice was like ice. 'I won't forget. I'll see to you later. Now get in there and get a deal.'

In the next minute or two, Beth saw at close quarters just why Richard Cross was a successful man. In the second it took to reopen the door of the boardroom, his dark fury turned again to warmth and charm. 'It is the prerogative of genius to be late,' he said to those seated around the table. 'This is our youngest and best account manager, Beth Forrester.'

As the visitors stood up to be introduced, Richard whispered to Beth, 'And it is the prerogative of the late to be a genius.' He then raised his voice and said, 'I'd like you to meet Chester Hampton, the founder and managing director of Internat.'

Beth knew she did not stand a chance. She had totally forgotten about the meeting, had not prepared, and would much rather be crying in the toilet. She looked at Chester Hampton. He had a kind face, the shy, bookish look of an academic, and he appeared surprisingly young for someone so incredibly successful. She would talk directly to him.

As she opened her briefcase at one end of the table, she tried to recall what she knew about Internat. The company was a sensation in the already sensational world of information technology, a by-word for overnight success and brilliant thinking. Hampton himself had come up with not one but two remarkable pieces of software, both unique and wanted by every user who ever switched on a computer. Every advertising agency in the western world wanted Internat's business and here the founder was, sitting along the table from her with an expectant look on his face.

Beth wished the floor would open up and swallow her. None of what she remembered helped her; in fact it made things worse. It made her realise how little she knew and how much she should have prepared.

But it was too late now.

'What can Cross, Carstairs and Denton do for Internat?' she began rhetorically. 'Well, the best way I can inform you is to tell you what we have done and are doing for Rybix Limited…'

She sensed Richard Cross frowning, but ploughed on blindly. For half an hour, not always coherently, she explained the campaign she and her colleagues had drawn up for Rybix. She took out her folder of photographs from the previous day's shoot and spread them over the table for Hampton and his colleagues to see. She explained how they would be used on posters and press advertisements, and how a separate television advertising campaign was being planned.

At the end of the half hour she stuttered to a halt, trying to mask her lack of anything further to say by reaching for a glass of water. After an anxious sip, she concluded lamely, 'You can see that we always give one hundred per cent to everything we do.'

As she sat down, sincerely wishing she were somewhere else, Richard stood up. 'Thank you, Beth, for the concise account of what we can and are doing for another client,' he said cuttingly, and then turned his attention to Hampton and the others. 'Of course, what we would do for Internat would be totally unique, and unlike any other campaign we've run.'

For ten minutes or so he spoke fluently and apparently extemporaneously. He described a campaign on both sides of the Atlantic that would, first and foremost, use the singular properties of the internet itself, supplemented by a highly organised but apparently impromptu word of mouth whispering campaign in London and New York.

'The best advertising,' he concluded, 'is advertising that the client does not have to pay for and the customer does not realise he is getting.'

With that, a member of staff popped a champagne cork, and drinks were offered around. The dozen or so people in the room stood up, stretching their limbs and reaching for their suit jackets and drinks. The informal negotiations were starting, the getting-to-know-you period between members of each side.

Beth gathered up the photographs from the table, stuffing them back into the folder.

'Thank you, Ms Forrester.' She looked up to see Chester Hampton alongside her. 'It was good to learn what you're doing for another company.'

She pushed her hair out of her eyes with an impatient gesture. 'You are being sarcastic, I presume,' she replied, somewhat belligerently, unsuccessfully trying to suppress the self-annoyance she felt.

'No, I assure you, not at all.' Hampton seemed taken aback by her aggressive tone. 'I mean it. I was genuinely interested to hear what you are doing for another company.' He smiled warmly. 'It's all Greek to me; I am fairly new in business.'

Beth chuckled. 'Not that new, I gather,' she said, trying to imagine how it must feel to have his millions, but as soon as she said it, as she heard her own words, she rebuked herself. Why was she being so rude? The poor man was trying to be nice, despite the whole crappy presentation being her fault, and her fault alone. She was only making things worse, and being unnecessarily rude to a major client who seemed prepared to overlook her lack of professionalism and was trying to be nice. She glanced across the room and caught Richard's eye. His slow, almost imperceptible shake of the head reinforced what she was feeling. He was warning her.

'You look fairly new yourself,' Hampton was saying. 'You are very young to hold such an important position.'

Beth hardly heard what he was saying; she was so flustered by the expression on Richard's face. In her confusion she dropped the folder she was holding, and some photographs spilled out onto the floor, face down. She quickly bent to scoop them up, almost banging heads with Hampton, who politely knelt to help her.

He retrieved two and glanced at them before handing them back. As she took them from his hand she noticed a blush on his cheeks, and looking at the photographs as she replaced them in her folder, she realised with horror that they were of her naked and glowing bottom.

Richard Cross was approaching them with a determined stride. He had seen the folder fall and was obviously not amused.

Beth felt she owed Hampton some sort of explanation. 'Um, those are for a different campaign,' she said with a nervous, unconvincing laugh. 'More hard-hitting, gritty realism. That sort of stuff.'

But before Hampton could reply, Richard Cross took her by the arm. 'Beth, you have another appointment, don't you,' he stated, squeezing her wrist painfully to emphasise his words, so she shook hands with Hampton and gathered up her bag, preparing to go.

'And don't forget you have an appointment with me later,' Richard added, his voice neutral. 'In my office.'

Beth hurried along the street, her mood now the opposite of what it had been a while earlier. She cursed herself. She had been going to use the previous evening for research into Internat, to prepare a presentation. And then Celeste had to come home as 'Charlie', and from that moment they both had other things on their minds. It was all Celeste's fault. Of course it was. But that was no real excuse, and did not make things better with her boss. Perhaps the second present she was now seeking to buy for him would help. Perhaps, but it was unlikely.

At about five o'clock she knocked on Richard's office door carrying a strangely shaped package beneath one arm. On hearing a muffled, 'Come in,' she entered to find her boss sitting behind his desk doing some paperwork.

'About time,' he said grimly, putting down his pen, and then added, 'What on earth is that?' indicating the package. 'Let me guess,' he went on. 'It's a metal detector.'

Beth looked down at the wrapping paper. It could be a metal detector, she thought. It had a long thin handle and a heavy square end. 'It's a present for you,' she said.

'A present?' Helen Cross turned from the window, a drink in her hand. 'Look, Richard, the little darling's brought you a present. Isn't that sweet?'

Beth, who had been unaware of Helen's presence until she spoke, quickly put the package on the desk.

'Why would I want a metal detector?' Richard queried, then looked at his wife. 'Darling, you remember Beth

Forrester, don't you?'

'Of course I do, though I hardly recognised her with her clothes on,' Helen snorted patronisingly, easing gracefully down onto the leather office couch.

'So,' Richard addressed Beth again, 'do I get my present now?'

Beth glanced at Helen, who was sipping her gin and tonic. 'Not now, Richard,' she said. 'Perhaps some other time—'

'Yes, now, I think,' Helen interrupted. 'I'm intrigued.'

'Please, Richard, not now,' Beth said, looking pointedly at Helen. 'It's not... it's not appropriate. I didn't realise... I thought we would be alone.'

'Now I *am* intrigued,' Helen scoffed. 'We must open it straightaway, mustn't we, Richard?'

'Yes, Beth,' Richard said, 'I think you should open it.'

Reluctantly, with shaking fingers, Beth unwrapped one end of the parcel and slid out a long, thin bamboo stick. It had a red ribbon tied in a bow at one end, holding a gift card.

'Goodness! A cane, Richard, for you.' Helen smiled wolfishly at her husband, rose gracefully, and approached the desk. 'I have always said a man can't have too many canes, haven't I?' She turned to Beth. 'And whom is he supposed to use it on? Let me look,' she added, and snatched at the ribbon and card.

Before Beth could object the haughty woman studied the greeting and then passed it to her husband. 'How sweet,' she purred. 'She has written you a poem.'

Without looking at the card, Richard passed it straight to Beth. 'You read it.'

Beth felt terrible and stuttered apologetically. 'It – it was supposed to b-be for you alone... I didn't have much time to think of a message.'

'Just read it,' he said, flexing the cane.

'*To Richard...*' she mumbled, with a halting voice. 'Please, must I go on?'

'Yes,' he insisted ruthlessly, 'you must.'

'The hand of the new owner
May discover its many uses
On the bottom of the donor
If and whenever he chooses.'

Helen tittered theatrically, and Richard cut the cane through the air, grinning sardonically.

'It needs a little work, I think, Beth,' he mused critically. 'Actually, I've a poem too that I'm sure you will like, even though it isn't mine.

'A woman, a spaniel and a walnut tree; the more you beat them the better they be.'

Beth smiled politely, puzzled by the ditty.

Richard swished the cane again. 'Judging by the shape of the present, this is not all you've bought me.'

Beth tried to make light of it. 'That's all for now,' she said.

'No,' said Helen. 'I insist. You came bearing gifts so you must deliver them. Don't mind me.'

Beth could tell by Richard's expression that he agreed with his wife, so she burrowed into the paper wrapping again and extracted the picture frame, gleaming in the evening light. Quietly she handed it to him, and his wife moved beside his chair to look over his shoulder.

Together they studied the photograph. It was of Beth, naked apart from the diamond pendant and high heels, facing the camera. Her head was bowed, her hands lightly clasped in front of her pubis and one foot slightly in front of the other.

'Well, it's lovely,' Richard said, apparently sincerely.

'It's a cheek,' Helen expostulated. 'You've got a nerve, young lady,' she said curtly to Beth. 'What's he supposed to do with it, take it home and put it by our bed?'

Beth appealed to Richard. 'I'm sorry,' she said. 'I thought you would like it. I imagined you might put it in a drawer in the office here. It was supposed to be a joke between you and me, and a little thank you for giving me the chance to secure the Rybix deal.' She looked from one to the other. 'I didn't think,' she said meekly, 'I'm truly sorry.'

'You mean you didn't think that I'd be here,' Helen accused, turning to her husband. 'Well, Richard, what are you going to do about such provocative behaviour from one of your employees?'

'First things first,' he said mildly to his wife. 'I have a bone to pick with her.' He looked up at Beth, his expression stern. 'Rybix is one thing, but you do realise you have almost cost us the Internat contract, don't you?'

Beth nodded contritely. 'Yes, Richard, and I'm very sorry—'

'And…?'

Beth knew what was coming, where he was leading her. 'And… and I deserve to be punished for my total lack of professionalism earlier, and for letting myself, you, and the company down,' she said quietly. 'I deserve to be severely punished.'

'I think we all agree on that,' he confirmed, slowly nodding, then looked at his wife. 'But how best to do it appropriately?'

A crafty smile spread over Helen's face. 'I'll have to

think,' she said, 'and I can't think with her standing there.' She waved a hand at Beth. 'While we give this due deliberation I'd prefer her to stand in the corner. That's what normally happens to recusant girls.'

Beth looked at Richard, and he nodded, so she started to walk to one corner of the office, when Helen spoke again.

'Naked,' she said, and Richard nodded again.

Beth was aghast. 'But, what happens if someone comes in?' she protested meekly. 'There are still people in the building.'

'Then they'll be surprised, and perhaps pleasantly surprised,' Helen said. 'Now, naked.'

Beth tried to console herself that neither of them had mentioned her getting the sack. As quickly as possible she stripped off her suit, blouse and bra. Then she hesitated with her hands on the waistband of her knickers.

'Completely naked,' Helen reiterated.

Beth abandoned any attempt at modesty. She levered off her shoes and slid down her knickers, stepping out of them, and then moved to the corner, away from Helen and Richard, alongside the door through which she had entered a few minutes before.

'Face the wall,' Helen instructed, and Beth turned to face the corner, silently cursing the older woman.

'Now, Richard,' Beth heard Helen say. 'What are we...?'

Her question was interrupted by a knock on the door, and Beth felt she was going to die of shame. The door opened, and just its thickness separated her and whoever stood on the other side of it.

'Sorry to interrupt, Richard,' a male said. 'Oh, hello Helen, I didn't realise it was you. Anyway, just to let you know I'm off now, so I'll see you when I get back from my trip.'

Beth shivered as she recognised the voice. It was Mark Truscott, a young account manager. She pressed herself against the wall, tight into the corner, and silently implored Richard not to ask him in.

'Okay, Mark,' she heard her boss say. 'Busy evening planned?'

'Yes,' the voice behind the door replied. 'A poker night.'

'I didn't know you played,' Richard said conversationally, as Beth silently begged him to make the account manager go.

'I don't, but my wife does, every Wednesday. I have to look after the kids.'

'Good for you,' Richard chuckled. 'And good luck in Geneva tomorrow.'

'Thanks; I'll tell you how it went as soon as I get back. Well, goodnight.'

The door started to close, and Beth was about to breathe normally again when she heard Richard call out, 'Oh, Mark,' and the door swung open again. Oh no, Richard was playing a cruel game and was going to invite him in after all.

'Is there anyone else out there?' her boss asked.

'No,' Mark said. 'I'm the last. I'll lock up on my way out. The cleaners will be here soon, but they have their own keys.'

'Yes, of course they do,' Richard said. 'Okay, fine,' and the door closed quietly.

'That was almost fun,' Beth heard Helen say. She felt weak with relief and put both hands on the wall to support herself.

'And now to business, my darling,' Helen said to her

130

husband, and Beth heard her approaching from behind and then felt the woman's hand on her shoulder. 'Our little troublemaker is getting cold,' she said. 'We must warm her up a little.' The hand slid down Beth's back and over the soft curves of her bottom.

'Yes, we must,' Richard said.

'She is very beautiful, I have to admit,' Helen mused, turning Beth by pushing her hip. 'And it is a beauty that should be shared. Look here.' She pinched the nipple nearest her between thumb and forefinger. 'And here.' She pushed her hand between Beth's legs and cupped the lips of her sex. 'Everyone should see this. I am sure Mark Truscott would have liked a look.'

'But we can hardly parade her through the office,' Richard objected. 'Besides, there's no one there.'

'No, but there is a photograph, and a very revealing photograph.' As she spoke, Helen ran one finger back and forth against Beth's warm, moist labia. 'She was shameless in giving it to you. She'd probably appreciate a wider audience for it.'

'Yes,' Richard concurred, a cunning glint in his eye. 'I could post it on the company notice board.'

'What an exquisite idea,' said Helen, thrusting her finger into Beth's warm softness.

'Oh, no,' Beth gasped. 'Please no, Richard, the photograph was for you.'

'Please no, Richard,' Helen mocked, rotating her finger, 'the photograph was for you.'

Beth looked into the cruel woman's eyes. 'Please, Helen, not that. Do anything you want, but not that. I would rather be thrashed for the way I behaved earlier.'

'Did you hear that, Richard?' the woman called over her shoulder, her eyes never leaving Beth's. 'She would rather be thrashed in front of the staff.'

'No, I didn't say that,' Beth spluttered, almost in tears. 'I meant I would rather be thrashed by you – by both of you.'

'Mm, you'll be thrashed all right,' Helen said, withdrawing her finger and spitefully pinching the tender inside of one of Beth's thigh, making the girl squeal miserably. 'Hm, she's somewhat squeamish,' she sneered.

'Now, come here, girl,' Helen commanded, and Beth turned and followed the woman to the desk.

'She's a troublesome girl,' Helen said to Richard, 'and it is definitely time for her to feel the cut of the cane.' She pressed Beth between the shoulders, and the girl had no choice but to bend forward and lean on the desktop, submissively presented before her seated boss. He surveyed the delicious site she presented for him, and then rose solemnly. There was a muffled exchange behind her, she heard the cane whistle viciously threw the air, and then her head jerked up from the polished mahogany surface and she had to clench her teeth to stop herself from crying out as the crack of the implement against her taut flesh resonated around the plush room. A searing pain bit across both buttocks and her whole body froze into tense rigidity, her eyes clamped as tightly shut as her jaw.

And so Beth was punished. Six times she heard the chilling sound and felt the scalding bite, and six times she jerked on the solid desk and suppressed the scream that threatened to wrench from her lungs.

When it was over her forehead rested on the top, silent tears dripping onto the blotting pad and spreading outward. Through conflicting emotions she for some reason wondered if the cleaners were in the building yet, and if so, whether they had heard her shameful chastisement.

A warm hand was on her thighs, between them, stroking them and easing them farther apart. The same hand slid up, making a slippery furrow through the lips of her sex and on upwards until it reached her anus. She felt that most intimate flower of her person being teased and probed by a delicate finger. She closed her eyes, aware only of the burning sensations from her bottom and the sensations being induced by the intrusive finger.

She was frustrated when it withdrew, but she cried out when the cane again bit with unerring accuracy and force against her already scalding buttocks. Maybe it was because she had already been beaten once, or because of the short interlude, or because it was a different hand holding the cane, but the six new strokes were worse than the first. She sobbed aloud, not caring who heard, or saw.

When at last the fire was withdrawn, the warmth remained. Slowly, but in a now familiar manner, the warmth spread through her loins and belly, through and over her sex, and up her stomach to her breasts, squashed against the cool surface of the desk.

The finger returned, but this time it skewered her sex and flexed itself in the warm moisture within. It withdrew and she felt it spread that same moistness on her anus. Several times it travelled back and forth, and each time her bottom was made wetter with her own juices until, on the last return, the finger penetrated the tight ring it had lubricated so efficiently.

It dallied there for a while, embedded to the second knuckle, moving around inquisitively, and then withdrew again to be replaced at the tiny entrance a moment later by something warmer, softer and broader. Beth knew what it was. Richard had promised he would do it some day, and today was the day, now was the moment.

Despite being highly aroused, it was hard for Beth to relax, knowing that Helen Cross was observing everything she and her husband did. Then warm hands grasped her by the hips, one each side, as the firm but flexible shaft pushed at Beth's previously unopened backdoor. It was not to be denied by her chagrin or tightness. With one strong thrust her resistance was overcome, and Richard gained entry where no man had been sheathed before. Beth gasped and her back arched, lifting her breasts from the desk, astonished at the depth of her feelings.

If her body had initially resisted the invader, it was just as fierce in holding him there now her resistance was overcome. Her sphincter muscles clamped the penis in place, proving to be a far stronger vice than that of the muscles of her vagina. Slowly he used the weight of his body to ease himself forward, forcing his way deeper into Beth's soul. She closed her eyes, tears wet on her cheeks, oblivious now to all around her. His long slow thrust was halted only when his groin pressed against the punished flesh of her buttocks, his body heat making the weals burn yet again, and Beth suspected that no one, no thing, could ever possess her as she was being possessed at that moment.

Slowly, even gently, he began to ease himself back and forth. At the same time his fingers slid round her hips to the front, pressing between her thighs and the desk, combing through her pubic hair, gently pulling apart the lips of her sex. Two fingers from one hand stroked the eager nub of her clitoris, while two from the other hand plunged deep inside her.

He pumped back and forth, with each thrust slapping

his groin against the sore cheeks of her bottom, and grinding his fingers deeper into her sex. Beth knew it could not last long. Her whole body felt like liquid; molten lava before it erupts. At the second she knew her climax was coming it would not be denied, but the vigour of his movements was such that he slipped out of her grasping insides. Beth whimpered low in her throat, feeling robbed of a precious prize. Moments later it was back, firmer and more rigid than before. Again fingers combed through her pubic hair until they found her swollen clitoris. Beth gave herself over once again to the pulsing movement in her bottom and the probing in her sex. The volcano erupted with what felt like a thunderclap, sending seismic shockwaves shooting through her body.

What seemed an eternity later – to Beth, at least – she raised her head and opened her eyes. It seemed amazing that the world was still in the same place, and she felt too drained to move from where she sprawled.

No words were spoken; none were needed. The only sound in the room was that of combined, strained breathing.

Eventually Helen Cross did disturb the heavy silence that draped across the scene. 'I'm feeling quite jealous,' she said with a melodramatic sulk, her manicured fingers moving to the fastening of her skirt, 'and as recompense for the use of my husband, I think it only fair that you, little missy, show your appreciation and do something about it…'

Chapter Ten

Beth savoured the last spoonful of her lobster bisque and daintily dabbed her lips with the crisply laundered white napkin. She looked around, admiring the trappings and pleasures of wealth, or at least of a generous expense account. The well spaced tables covered in heavy white linen and gleaming silver; the willing but not obsequious waiters; the trolleys of roasted meats and creamy puddings; the dim lighting and the well dressed clientele. And Beth did not doubt that she belonged. A year ago she would have pretended and felt uncomfortable; now she felt entitled to all this and more.

She brought her gaze back to the man across the table and found him looking at her. 'It was very good of you to invite me to lunch, Chester,' she said sweetly. 'I did not expect it. To be frank, I did not even expect to see you again.'

He broke some bread on his plate. 'I'll be frank, too,' he said with a shy smile. 'I don't like those artificial boardroom meetings, total strangers trying to impress each other – trying to impress me. I would not employ anyone for any job unless I knew him or her, personally. If I have learned nothing else in the last two or three years, I have learned that.'

'Don't take people at face value?' Beth asked.

He nodded. 'Something like that. Maybe I am just a bad judge of character, but I do need time to get to know someone before I can trust them.'

Beth did not need her female intuition to get the message. Over her sole Veronique and his steak and kidney pudding, she gently quizzed him about his upbringing and his private life. More than enough had already been published about the public face of Chester Hampton.

He had been born in Norwich but was taken at the age of seven by his parents to Philadelphia, where his father took up an academic post. Chester was an only child, left largely to his own devices in a strange and alien world. Even before puberty he already showed an aptitude for electronic communication, and by the age of fourteen, he boasted with a shy smile, he had hacked into the CIA's mainframe at Langley, Virginia.

'A life of crime beckoned?' Beth teased, and was amused that Chester took her seriously. He shook his head solemnly.

'I thought I could make more money going straight,' he said openly.

'And you seem to have been right,' she said, refilling his glass with chilled champagne. 'Do you get a chance to spend any of your money?'

'I have a yacht moored on the Potomac.'

'And a crew of six blondes, I bet,' Beth teased again.

'One of them is blond, but he's a man. As are the other two.'

'So there is no Mrs Hampton, or Mrs Hampton-to-be?'

He shook his head, but as Beth studied the dessert menu, the question hung in the air. He dabbed his mouth too, and then fussed with the napkin, putting it first on his lap and then beside his plate.

'No dessert for me, thank you, Beth.' He paused while coffee cups magically appeared and coffee was poured. 'That's what I wanted to talk to you about, why I thought we should meet alone.'

Beth looked puzzled. He fiddled with the sugar bowl and the coffee spoon and it dawned on her that he was nervous, maybe even embarrassed.

'I don't go out much on my own because people recognise me,' Chester said. 'I don't get a chance to meet people, just as me.'

She nodded encouragingly, whilst smiling to herself; and incredibly rich man and he needed encouragement to open his mouth and talk.

'So, how can I help?' she prompted.

He sipped his coffee and dabbed his lips again. 'The photographs yesterday,' he said. 'There is a girl I would like to meet.' She smiled openly this time, and he rushed on trying to cover his embarrassment. 'It could be the prelude to an advertising campaign,' he gabbled, 'if I liked her—'

'But not necessarily a prelude to an advertising campaign, hm, Chester?' Beth interrupted, still smiling.

'Um, no, not necessarily,' he admitted. 'More like a date at first; a blind date, if you like.'

She placed her hand on top of his on the table. 'That might be possible,' she said gently, trying to soothe him. 'I'll see what I can do, but no promises.'

'Of course,' he burbled, 'I know this is highly unorthodox, asking you, perhaps even unethical.'

She patted his hand. 'It's okay, Chester. Really, I don't mind. No one need know. Which of the four did you like the most?'

He frowned. 'Four?'

'The four in the Rybix photographs,' she said patiently, teasing him without mercy. 'Which of them did you like?'

'Oh, no, not them,' he said, looking even more

embarrassed. 'The one in that other campaign you mentioned.' When Beth appeared confused, he added furtively, 'The one in the photographs you dropped on the floor.'

'Oh,' Beth said. She stared at him for a full ten seconds, and then picked up her briefcase and handbag. 'You must excuse me, Chester; I need to powder my nose. I'll be back in a sec.'

In the toilet cubicle, with the door locked, she opened again the folder of photographs from the previous day. The two Chester Hampton had picked up should still be at the bottom of the pile. She slid them out and stared at them. One showed her standing with her back to the camera, her bottom, picked out by a spotlight, glowing a bright, rosy red, with the rest of her seductively shaded. The other showed her bottom in close-up, the marks of Celeste's spanking clearly visible. So he liked spanking, she thought, and he clearly did not realise the photographs were of her.

'Sorry about that, Chester,' she said, back at the table. 'Where were we?'

'The girl in the photographs.'

Beth realised she needed to play for time, to gain time to think. 'I don't know much about her, Chester. I could find out and let you know. How long are you in town?'

'I leave the day after tomorrow,' he said. 'If you do this for me, Beth, I shan't forget it.'

She shook her head. 'I don't know, Chester. She's a top model, and very hard to get hold of.'

'I only want a date,' he persevered. 'One night, on her terms. And I can pay for her company.'

'She'd be silly to say no, if she's in town,' Beth said reassuringly. 'I'll let you know.'

Beth telephoned him late that afternoon. 'Can I talk, Chester?' she asked in a conspiratorial whisper.

'Yes, go ahead. I'm alone.'

'She's agreed to meet you.'

'Good!' he enthused. 'Excellent!'

'I told her that you'd seen her in the photographs.'

'Good.'

'I told her which photographs specifically; the ones that showed her bottom. After that she sounded even more interested.'

'Excellent! Where? When?'

'Before we get on to that, Chester, she wants to make some conditions.'

'Oh, yes, well as I said before, I can pay for her time.'

'No, it's not that, Chester. She is well known and wants to remain anonymous. She does not want you to know who she is.'

'How can we do that? She can't go out wearing a mask.'

'That's the point. She does not want to go out. She wants to meet you in your hotel suite. You could book the suite next to you for her. Book it in my name for tomorrow evening.'

'Yes, good, even better.'

'I'll bring her there myself. Just to make sure you find each other.'

'Yes, fine. Beth, I won't forget this.'

'Oh, Chester, one other thing. I think she's quite naughty. She likes games. I didn't think you would mind. She wants to know whether you would like her in a costume.'

'In a costume? Well, I hadn't really thought about it that—'

'So why not think about it now? What sort of girls do you like?'

'I… er… I have always liked cheerleaders. You know, American cheerleaders.'

'Then I'll tell her. See you tomorrow.'

'Oh, Beth, what do I call her?'

'Anything you like. What would you like to call her, Chester?'

'Um, Candy.'

'Candy. That's cute. Candy and I will be there tomorrow at nine.'

On the top floor of the exclusive hotel in London's West End, the carpet in the corridor was deep and plush, and Beth approached the door of suite fifty-one without a sound. It was eerily quiet, no people, no activity at all, just the faint hum of air conditioning. Whatever was happening behind all those closed doors, Beth thought, it would not matter, no one else would hear, the walls were so reassuringly substantial.

She knocked quietly on the door, not wanting to break the quiet, and Chester Hampton opened it almost immediately. He was in shirtsleeves and trousers, but his feet were bare and his hair was wet. He had apparently just come out of the shower. He shook her by the hand and led her inside.

'She's here, next door,' Beth said, cocking her head towards the adjoining suite.

Hampton looked pleased and excited, but most of all relieved. She realised that he probably doubted whether Candy would turn up. 'Thank you, Beth,' he said, grasping her hand again and giving it a squeeze.

'Remember the rules,' she went on. 'She'll be masked and she probably won't talk. She doesn't want you to know who she is. She is doing this for me and for the excitement.' She lowered her voice. 'She might be married for all you know, Chester. You don't want to cause her problems, do you.'

He shook his head solemnly. 'And what can I do with her?' he asked.

Beth smiled at him, amused by his puppy-like eagerness. 'Anything you want, within reason. She's a very naughty girl, I know that much. She likes games. Most games. If I know her, she'll leave it all up to you. She likes masterful men.'

Chester straightened his shoulders, obviously pleased by the reply.

Beth turned towards the door. 'Give us five minutes together, Chester, and then she'll be here. Make sure that door is unlocked.' She pointed to the internal door connecting the two suites. 'I'll be next door but don't worry; I won't interfere. I'll call back when Candy has left. You haven't got all night because she has to get home; she has a busy day tomorrow.'

Back in her own suite Beth undressed and dressed as quickly as she could while still taking pains to make everything just right. Several minutes later, she leaned over the dressing table to brush on a glossy red lipstick and to slip a white cat mask over her eyes, and then stood up to look at herself in the full length wall mirror.

She liked the look of Candy; she reminded her of an adolescent fantasy figure from her teenage years. As an English schoolgirl, she had often dreamed of being the sort of American co-ed she saw on television. Beth looked carefully at the figure in the mirror from top to toe. Candy wore white mid-calf boots but otherwise her legs were bare, almost to the tops of her thighs. Above was a very short, white pleated skirt and a loose white woollen jumper with a huge red letter A sewn on the front. Apart from the lipstick, her face looked scrubbed, pink with good health and, with the eyes masked, mischievously mysterious. Her blonde hair was caught up in two bangs on either side of her head. She twirled around, looking back over her shoulder, and caught a glimpse of the tight white knickers beneath her skirt. She smiled, showing perfect white teeth. Chester should like Candy. She picked up her hat, a white shako with a red star on the front, and tucked it under her arm. 'Ready,' she said softly to the mirror, taking a deep breath. 'Let's go.'

She knocked on the adjoining door with the padded tip of her twirling baton, and Chester Hampton opened it, looking the same as he had ten minutes earlier. 'You must be Candy,' he said, a little shyly. 'Please, come in.'

He closed the door and led her to the centre of his huge sitting room. 'Let me have a look at you,' he said, sitting in an easy chair. She stood before him, one knee slightly bent while he looked her up and down. 'Now the other side – turn round.'

She did as she was told, standing still until he spoke again.

'You know why you are here, don't you, Candy? I am told that you have been slacking in the cheerleading class.' She hung her head. 'I am also told that you have been fooling around with some members of the football team, but we'll get to that later. First, I'd like to see you go through your paces. March up and down for me.'

She marched back and forth in front of him from one wall to the other, lifting her knees extravagantly, like a high-stepping horse in a dressage contest. She felt her skirt lift with each step and she knew that the white of her knickers would show tantalisingly.

'Fine,' he said, as she began to flag. 'Now, let's try leaping. Some good high cheerleading leaps, if you please.'

Standing facing him, she leapt in the air, her arms and legs wide, her head thrown back. After the third leap he stood up and walked around behind her. 'Keep going,' he said. After three more leaps she stopped, gasping for breath.

'You are out of shape and you are not very supple,' he said. 'It just won't do.' He sat down again in front of her. 'Let me see you touch your toes.'

She raised her arms above her head and swung them down to the floor. Her feet were slightly apart, but she could feel the muscles and tendons on the backs of her thighs stretching. 'Keep going,' he said, rising again and walking around behind her. 'There's a lot of work yet to do.'

Again she swung downwards, trying to reach her toes. 'Hold it there,' he said from behind. 'It's good for the muscles to stretch like that.' She knew it was not just her muscles that were stretched, but her knickers too. She could feel them as taut as a drum skin across her bottom.

'We need to work on that position,' he said. 'Have a rest and then we'll get back to it. Show me some baton twirling in the meantime.'

Beth was glad to be standing upright again. She picked up the baton and tried to twirl it between her fingers. She was hopeless and she knew it. After she dropped it for the fourth time, Chester picked it up.

'There's more than one use for a stick like this,' he said pensively, running one hand up and down its length. 'And I can certainly think of one way to use it.'

She hung her head again. 'Get your breath back,' he went on. 'Have a drink. And then we'll start again, only this time in earnest,' he said, pouring her a coke in a tall glass. She drank it gratefully.

When she put the glass back on the table, he continued. 'Now, I think you should take your panties off. They seem to be restricting your movement.' She did as she was told, peeling them off and placing the delicate little white bundle alongside the glass.

'Let me see you leap again.'

She leapt in the air as before, head back, arms and legs apart and her skirt flying up to her waist. 'Your legs should be wider apart,' he ordered. Three times more she leapt as high as she could. 'Now touch your toes,' he commanded, without allowing her to stop for breath. He prowled around, studying her from all sides but particularly from behind, as she swung her arms high in the air and down as far as her boots. 'Lower,' he said.

When he finally allowed her to stand upright again, her cheeks were flushed and she was panting. 'You look hot,' he said. 'Take off your sweater.'

Grasping the hem, she lifted it carefully over her head, and then stood in front of him again in only her boots, skirt and mask. Her head was hanging down and she saw her small nipples, standing proud on her breasts.

For at least ten more minutes he made her do a series of exercises; bending, flexing, leaping and falling back on her hands to make a bridge. Finally she collapsed on her stomach on the floor, exhausted and with her skirt up around her waist, her bottom fully exposed and her legs apart.

'You are unfit and lazy,' he pronounced, standing over her. 'So now I am going to show you how we deal with that. Come here, and lie over my lap.'

He sat on an upright chair beside the table and she

lowered herself across his legs. With one hand he folded up her skirt and began to stroke the delicious naked bottom in front of him. She was glad to be still and relatively relaxed; all that leaping about had been truly exhausting.

He began to spank her, not hard at first but thoroughly, covering every inch of flesh from the creases at the top of her thighs to the dimples in the small of her back. She could feel the heat from the spanking and knew that her bottom would be glowing red, as it had been in the photographs.

For a while he stopped spanking her, only to pull gently at her flesh with his fingers, revealing first her sex and then her anus. Then the spanking resumed, harder and more painfully.

'Now I am going to teach you another use for that baton,' he said in due course, his voice tight with emotion. 'I want you to stand up and touch your toes again, and every time you try I shall offer encouragement.' As he spoke his fingers were undoing the catch on her skirt, so that when she stood up it shimmered to the floor.

Again she stood in the centre of the room with him behind her. She swung her arms up and then down. As her fingertips touched her boots he brought the short stick down across her buttocks. 'Lower,' he said, over and over again. The exercise and the beating seemed to last for ages. The baton was too short to hurt much, but she knew her bottom would be heavily striped. He was panting almost as hard as she was.

Suddenly it stopped and he resumed his seat, leaving her bent double. When he had recovered his composure he told her to stand in front of him.

'Now there's the question of your misbehaviour with

146

members of the football team,' he said. He raised the baton and touched her nipples with the round, padded end. 'Have any boys seen these?' he asked, and she nodded. He put the baton between her legs, and rubbed it back and forth against her sex. 'And this?' She shook her head. 'Are you sure?' he persisted, rubbing faster and probing between her moist lips. She shook her head again, her blonde locks swaying back and forth. He pushed his arm forward so that the end of the baton slid between her legs and up into the crease of her bottom. 'How about this?' he asked, and she shook her head vehemently. 'Then it must be this,' he said, raising the now damp baton to her lips and patting them. 'Suck it.' She opened her mouth and took the end of the baton inside, as if sucking a large lollipop.

'Show me what you do to the quarterback,' he said, putting the baton to one side. She leaned forward and unbuttoned his shirt, then helped him to stand. She undid his belt and zip and pushed down his trousers and underpants, putting them neatly to one side. She pushed him back into the chair and knelt before him. She ran her tongue along the flesh of his upper thighs until it could go no higher. With both hands she lifted his scrotum and began to lick the wrinkled sac, rubbing her warm cheek against his penis. Opening her lips wide, she gently took his testicles into her mouth, moving her tongue from side to side and around the tightening balls. Letting them go, she traced with the tip of her tongue the line from his scrotum, up the soft vein running the length of his penis to the shiny, purple head. She twirled it around the helmet and poked it into the tiny slit before opening her lips and swallowing all of the head and half the shaft. Slowly, very slowly so that he would get maximum enjoyment, she moved her head up and down, filling her mouth with warm saliva to lubricate him. With each movement she swallowed a little more of him, taking his rigid penis deeper and deeper into her throat.

He slumped back and closed his eyes, waiting for the inevitable that was about to come. But as his muscles tensed and he began to pant, she stopped and pulled her face away.

'Don't stop,' he said, but she shook her head and clasped his penis with one hand. 'I said don't stop.'

She shook her head again, and began to move her hand up and down the shaft.

'You might tease the lads in the football team like that,' he said, pushing her hand away, 'but you don't do it to grown men.' He reached forward and grasped the back of her head with both hands, pushing it back down into his lap. 'I want you to drink it,' and as she again took the purple plum into her mouth, he added, 'all of it.'

Seconds later she did just that, swallowing every drop of his ejaculation and licking her lips as she withdrew her head. He flopped in the chair with his eyes closed, deep slow breaths making his chest rise and fall as she quickly collected her clothes and left the room the same way she had come.

Beth again stood at the door of Chester Hampton's suite. She was wearing her business suit, familiar deep red lipstick and her hair was properly brushed.

'Candy has gone,' she told him, and she was not lying. 'Did you like her?'

Hampton looked ruffled but happy. 'Yes, very much,' he said. 'I can't think how to thank you.'

'I can,' she said, her eyes shining brightly.

'Well, for a start, you should stay in the suite,' he said, 'as it's all paid for. Enjoy a little luxury for the night.'

She waved the plastic key she was holding. 'Okay – good night then.'

As she turned he took her by the arm. 'Beth,' he said conspiratorially, 'I'll be back next week. Would it be possible to see Candy again?'

'It might be,' she teased, 'but it'll cost you.'

He smiled. 'Well I expect there's an easy way to pay my debt to Cross, Carstairs and Denton.'

'Yes,' she said, feeling very pleased with herself, 'there is. Good night, Chester.'

Beth sunk lower into the scented water of the bathtub feeling the bubbles erupt around her hips. She stretched out one leg and wiggled her toes between Celeste's thighs until they relaxed and opened to allow her access.

Celeste had arrived just twenty-two minutes after her call. 'Grab a toothbrush and come and join me in my luxury suite,' Beth said, adding, 'and don't worry about a nightie.'

Celeste slid forward in the tub so that her sex pressed against the ball of Beth's foot. 'Tell me all about it,' she said. 'Every detail, every inch,' she giggled.

After Beth had told her, Celeste asked, 'So is your bum sore?' When Beth nodded, Celeste said, 'So is mine. T.J. never leaves me alone. If it's not a spanking, it's the cane. And if it's not the cane, it's the slipper.'

Beth reached towards the shelf along the side of the bath. 'There should be something here among all these luxurious freebies that we can rub on each other.' She held up and studied a series of multi-coloured miniature bottles and sachets. 'Ah,' she said. 'Cold cream.'

Ten minutes later she was lying naked on her stomach on a huge bed with an equally naked Celeste kneeling beside her. 'Your poor bottom,' Celeste cooed, leaning forward to kiss and lick the punished flesh before slapping a dollop of cold cream between the cheeks.

'And yours,' Beth muttered into the counterpane, remembering her friend's buttocks as they had been a few minutes before when she dried and powdered them. The delicate skin was smudged with pink and purple blotches.

Celeste smoothed the cream over the two soft mounds and down into the valley between. 'We need someone else to help us take the strain, and the pain.'

'Mm,' Beth murmured, enjoying Celeste's touch. 'I've been thinking the same thing.' She opened her legs to allow Celeste greater access. 'There could be someone…'

Celeste smoothed the cream into the lips of Beth's sex. 'Oh? Tell momma.'

Beth raised her hips so that Celeste's finger slid inside, a place already so wet that no cream was needed. 'Well, I think the person I am thinking about might be one of us. I'll say no more for the moment. Just let your fingers do the talking for now.'

Chapter Eleven

Beth was on the telephone in the office talking to Peter Parnell. She thanked him effusively for the proofs of the Rybix shoot and asked him about his availability for another job. Just before saying goodbye, she asked casually, 'Peter, you don't have the home telephone number of Natasha Perry, do you?'

'Natasha who?'

'Perry. One of the girls in the Rybix shoot.'

'I've probably got it here somewhere,' he said. 'Why?'

'Because I need it, Peter. Would you have a look?'

'I will if you give me Charlie's number,' he said.

'Her name is not Charlie,' Beth retorted.

'She'll always be Charlie to me. Hang on, I'll go have a look.'

In less than a minute he was back with the number. 'Remember you owe me, Beth. Send Charlie around here on another errand. She's the sweetest creature I've ever met.'

Beth laughed. 'Don't be offended, Peter, but I think she likes her men just a touch more masculine than you.'

As soon as she'd said goodbye and put down the receiver, she picked it up again and dialled the number.

'Natasha Perry,' said the same bright voice that she recalled from before.

'Natasha, this is Beth – Beth Forrester from Cross, Carstairs and Denton. You probably don't remember me but we met—'

'I remember you well, Beth,' Natasha interrupted. 'Very well indeed… and I'm extremely glad you've called.'

'Oh, great,' Beth said, the promising tone of the girl's voice making her pulse quicken. 'Well forgive me telephoning you at home, I know I should go through your agent, but as this is just an exploratory call, I thought you wouldn't mind.'

'Not at all, Beth,' Natasha replied. 'I'm only too pleased to hear from you. I've thought a lot about the other day…'

Beth did not want to pursue that particular subject – not for now, at least. She tried to sound businesslike. 'Good, well, I'm planning, or at least thinking about a new and different campaign. I thought you might be very good for it. You've the right looks.'

'Sounds fascinating,' Natasha said brightly. 'I'm certainly game for anything. Things are rather quiet right now.'

'Excellent. So we should meet, just to discuss things.'

'Any time,' Natasha said. 'You say when and where, and I'll be there.'

'I noticed when I was calling you that you have the same telephone prefix as I have at home. Where do you live?'

'Pimlico.'

'Then we're neighbours,' Beth said. 'What are you doing tonight? How about coming to dinner.'

'Mm, I'd like that.'

'It won't be much,' Beth warned. 'Neither I nor my flatmate are cooks.'

Natasha laughed. 'I don't mind. I'll bring a bottle of cheap wine to kill the taste. What's the address and what time?'

At the appointed time that evening, Celeste called from the kitchen, 'So where is she?'

'Don't worry about it; she's always late,' Beth replied, just as the doorbell rang.

Natasha stood on the threshold holding out a bottle wrapped in tissue paper. Beth thought she looked adorable. Natasha was small and slender, dressed completely in black, in a polo-neck sweater, slacks and flat-soled shoes. Her black hair was loose and framed her face, curling inwards slightly under her chin.

Beth smiled her welcome. 'You don't look old enough to drink,' she said, taking the proffered bottle.

'You'd be surprised,' Natasha replied, walking into the sitting room.

Beth introduced Celeste and fussed around pouring drinks. After chatting for five minutes or so about the pros and cons of living in Pimlico, Celeste started to ask Natasha about her life as a model, but Beth cut her off in mid-sentence. 'Get back to the kitchen, wench,' she said playfully. 'I want to talk business with Natasha.'

Celeste pouted, but got up anyway. 'Remember, I can hear every word,' she said, disappearing around the corner.

To try to put her visitor at ease, Beth queried Natasha about herself and her background. 'Where does your family live?'

'I don't have any family,' Natasha replied bluntly.

Beth flushed, fearing she had entered forbidden territory. 'Do you live alone?'

'Yes, just two streets away.' Natasha looked around her. 'But it is pretty squalid; nothing like this. May I look around?'

'Don't show her my room,' Celeste called. 'She hasn't

even seen squalid until she's seen in there!'

When the two were sitting down again, with their second glass of wine, Beth spoke about business. She talked at length about marketing and advertising, the difficulties of being an account manager, the need for fresh thinking and originality in each campaign, how each message should be geared to the medium that would carry it and how client companies judged only by results.

Natasha listened carefully and when Beth stopped, she said, 'It sounds fascinating, and so much more interesting than my job. I am nothing more than a clotheshorse.'

Beth nodded. 'It is fascinating, but it is also very demanding,' she pointed out. 'It takes all my skills, everything I've got.'

She went on to explain that she was just thinking about a new campaign. It would be deliberately designed to shock, to command attention and to cause controversy, and would feature a series of photographs in underground magazines.

'Is that where I come in?' Natasha asked, sitting forward on the sofa, indicating her interest.

'Possibly,' Beth said. 'You wore a swimsuit in the studio for the ice cream shoot. Have you ever modelled underwear?'

'Yes,' Natasha confirmed. 'It's all the same to me.'

'You don't think it's degrading?'

'Not at all. Why should I? It's all money in the bank.'

Beth poured Natasha a third glass of wine. 'Would you consider posing in the nude or the semi-nude?' she asked.

Natasha smiled, looking directly into her eyes. 'Like you did the other day?'

Beth resumed her seat. 'I hoped that was not going to come up, but yes, something like that.'

Natasha stroked the stem of her glass. 'I would,' she said eventually. 'I am not certain my body is attractive enough though; not as attractive as yours, leastways.'

Beth waved a hand in the air dismissively, brushing Natasha's protest aside. 'We're not talking about me here. Anyhow, as far as I can see you've got a gorgeous figure. You shouldn't be so modest. Now, would you mind showing me?'

Natasha put down her glass. 'No, I don't think I would... now?'

When Beth nodded, she stood up and with natural sexiness pulled her sweater over her head and unfastened her waistband to wriggle her trousers down. Then she stood unselfconsciously in the centre of the room with her arms to her sides so that Beth could study her. She wore a low-cut brassiere and a g-string, both of them black. Beth was pleasantly surprised how full Natasha's breasts were, for someone so petit and slender. She had not really noticed the other day during the photo shoot and this evening they had, until now, been hidden under a loose sweater. Now they were standing full and proud, creamy flesh cradled in black lace.

Beth let her gaze roam downwards. The bikini style pants hid little other than the slight mound of the girl's sex. Her hips were gently rounded, her groin devoid of visible hair, the thighs slender and straight. Natasha obviously looked after herself, as a model always should.

There was the sound of a low wolf-whistle from the doorway and both girls looked round to see Celeste standing there with a saucepan in her hands. 'Not bad,' she announced approvingly, and then added quickly to Beth, 'It's okay, I'm going. I know my place,' before disappearing again.

Beth smiled an apology to Natasha. 'She's right; you're not bad... not bad at all.'

She rose and led Natasha to her bookshelves, which stretched from floor to ceiling against one wall, and placed her with her back to the books. 'Stand with your arms outstretched, feet together and head down,' she instructed.

Without another word Natasha adopted the pose, and Beth stood back to admire her model. 'Perhaps without your bra,' she decided.

Again without a word, Natasha unhooked the skimpy lace garment and threw it onto the sofa with the rest of her clothes, and then resumed the pose with her head bowed and her black hair falling loosely forward. Beth thought she looked stunning. The girl's breasts were even more beautiful than she had previously imagined, firm and proud with soft, pink nipples.

'Turn around, would you?' she said. 'Arms above your head.'

Natasha turned to face the books, raising her hands. Beth took a velvet tieback cord from one curtain and then stood on a chair to fasten Natasha's wrists above her head, tying them to a metal stanchion that supported the top shelf. 'Bondage,' Natasha purred, as Beth climbed down and stood back to admire the sensual tableau.

Her eyes travelled down Natasha's slender arms to her smooth back, its muscles stretched and the spine indented, to a waist so narrow Beth was sure she could span it with two hands. A dimple on either side marked the place where the waist flared out into a bottom as round as an apple, the two perfect cheeks divided by the neat black line of the girl's g-string.

Beth could not resist it. She let her hand run down the length of the valley of the girl's spine until it reached the

156

waistband of the g-string. 'You have glorious skin, so soft,' she said, clearing her throat a little as she spoke. 'Do you mind?' she added, hooking her fingers into the g-string.

When Natasha made no protest, Beth pushed it downwards, over the soft flesh and then down the girl's legs. As she worked them off Natasha's feet, she deliberately placed her cheek against the girl's bottom, feeling the soft warmth pass from flesh to flesh. With some difficulty she resisted the urge to kiss it.

'I'll take a quick snap with my digital camera so you can see,' she said, and she did, and then untied the girl, telling her to adopt the original pose. She used the viewfinder to study the innocent beauty from the front. Natasha's skin was as white and as unflawed as the best porcelain, made even whiter by the pink of her nipples and the shiny black of the tiny patch of pubic hair discreetly obscuring her sex.

'Beautiful,' Beth breathed, using the camera to study the photos she'd taken.

'Let me see,' Natasha said eagerly, and seemed totally unconcerned by her nakedness, both in digital form and in reality.

'Just one more,' Beth said, when Natasha leant down to put the camera on the coffee table.

'Let me guess,' Natasha said sexily. 'Would this last one have anything to do with corporal punishment? Is this how you want me, for example?'

She turned away from Beth and bent at the hips, grasping her knees with both hands. 'Isn't this the way you were the other day, Beth?' she said provocatively, looking back over her shoulder. 'Does it give you any ideas? It certainly gives me ideas.'

Beth said nothing. She stared at Natasha's lovely bottom and at her sex peeping between her parted thighs, the neat line dividing the moist lips that, it seemed to Beth, were pouting an invitation. She wanted to smack those buttocks and kiss those lips, but instead she put the camera to her eye and pressed the button.

'What do you think?' Natasha asked, when she was dressed again and sitting on the sofa, drinking more wine.

'I think you're gorgeous,' Beth said.

'Do you really?' Natasha replied thoughtfully. 'Then that explains it.'

'Explains what?'

Natasha sipped her drink. 'I've been posed like that before,' she admitted. 'Quite a few times, in fact, but I never knew what I looked like before. That's why I stared at you so much in Parnell's studio the other day. It must have annoyed you, but it brought back many memories for me.'

She lifted her feet and lay back on the sofa, closing her eyes with a deep sigh.

'Are you going to tell me then?' Beth gently prompted, after a minute's silence.

'Tell you what?' Celeste asked, entering the room. 'It's all cooking nicely. It'll be about half an hour,' she said, sitting down. 'Tell you what?'

Beth held a finger to her lips and nodded at Natasha, still lying with her eyes closed on the sofa. She was giving the girl time to think.

Finally, Natasha spoke, still not opening her eyes. 'It brought it all back,' she said, 'bending over in front of you.'

She sat up, her normal bubbly self slightly deflated. 'You asked me about my family. I never had a family; I never

158

knew my parents.' Beth and Celeste listened but said nothing, so Natasha went on.

'I was raised by foster parents in Kidderminster. When I was about eight they thought I was too difficult to cope with properly. They had other children in their care, so I was moved on to other foster parents and so on. Between the ages of eight and thirteen I had four sets of foster parents. It didn't make things better, you can imagine. I started to bunk off school, to smoke dope, things like that. I must have been pretty difficult.

Anyway, when I was thirteen I was placed in a hostel. It was like a remand home for kids who had been in trouble with the law.'

Natasha paused and drank some more wine. Celeste refilled her glass.

'To start with I quite liked it,' Natasha said, swirling the wine around in her glass. 'In a funny way, I had more freedom. I liked being with the other kids. Then two of the boys got into trouble, serious trouble, and the regime changed. A new warden was appointed and everything became much stricter. By now I was sixteen and doing really well at school. By and large I behaved myself; I wasn't interested in getting into trouble. But it didn't work out like that. The chief warden, Mr Chambers, used to pick on me. He was always telling me off for tiny things, mostly imaginary misdemeanours and mistakes. He just liked telling me off.'

She finished her wine in one gulp, and Celeste replenished all the glasses. 'Go on,' she said to Natasha. 'I didn't mean to interrupt.'

'One Sunday when the place was empty I came across him in the corridor. He stopped me and said he'd received a complaint from another girl that I wasn't showering often enough. It was a lie, of course; I used to shower every morning. I've always been very particular about cleanliness. I think he just made it up.

'Anyway, he told me to go and have a shower immediately. I said I already had and he said I should have another one. Then, when I was in the shower, the door opened and he was standing there. He said he had come to make sure I washed properly. He made me wash my breasts, then between my legs, front and back, over and over again, and after I'd dried myself he inspected me – far more closely than he should have.

'And that was the start of it. I wish now I had made a fuss at the time, reported him to someone, but I was too naïve and scared. After that, he used to pick on me all the time, usually when we were alone and no one else could see.

'A week or two later he told me that he had a bad report from my school and that I should report to him that evening in his office. It wasn't a bad report; it just wasn't one of my best. After that though, because of him, my schoolwork did begin to go downhill.

'Then one day, in his office, he told me he was going to punish me by spanking me. He made me lie over his lap and he turned up my skirt and pulled down my panties. I was crying even before he smacked me, I was so scared. It lasted a long time but he never hit me very hard. When it was all over I was extremely relieved. Then he told me to come back again the next evening, and when I went back he said he wanted to inspect the marks, to see if I was okay. He made me stand in front of him and pull down my panties. He poked and prodded me and then sent me away.

'Dirty bastard,' Celeste said, utterly engrossed in what

Natasha was confiding in them.

Natasha nodded. 'He was, and I was just too young to understand. To me he was an authority figure, someone to be obeyed. After that he used to find fault with me as often as he could and it was always the same routine. He would spank me one night, usually late at night after lights out, and I would have to go back the next evening to show him my bottom. Hardly a night went by when I did not have to bare my bottom in front of him – either for a spanking or for an inspection of the results of the previous spanking.

'And I used to hate the inspections more than the spanking. He got into the habit of making me lie over his lap for the assessment as if I was going to be spanked again. He never actually touched my sex, but he used to poke and prod me. He liked to run the palm of his hand round and round over my buttocks, pulling the cheeks of my bottom apart and asking me if it hurt. I have never told anyone this. Do you want me to go on?'

'Yes, we do,' Beth urged intensely, 'so long as you don't mind talking about it.'

'I suppose I guessed he was getting a kick out of it,' Natasha continued, 'but I wasn't that sure. I just didn't understand enough, until one night. I had left my books in his room and I ducked back in straight after a spanking, without knocking, and low and behold he was wanking. I caught him with his cock in his fist. He tried to cover up and yelled at me to get out, but he knew I knew what he was doing.'

Beth giggled and Celeste snorted into her drink, spilling wine down her front.

'It wasn't funny,' Natasha said. 'It made things worse. The next time he called me in, two days later, he was

161

different. The matron was there. He told me of my misdemeanour. I can't remember now what it was, but it was definitely something trivial. Then he said he was going to cane me. He made me take off my skirt and knickers and lie over his desk with my arms outstretched so that matron could hold me by the wrists. Then he caned me very hard, and I still had to go back for the inspection the following night. Matron was there again and this time I had to lie over her lap, naked from the waist down while Chambers watched. I was really sore from the cane, you can imagine, and she was not at all gentle. She slapped cream on my buttocks and rubbed it in roughly. I can still feel her stubby fingers pushing and probing, her nails digging into me.

'It went on like that until I was old enough to leave; every time the welts would fade he would find some excuse to punish me again.'

Natasha stopped talking and picked up the camera again, eyeing the digital image of herself bending over. 'That's why I wanted to see this, to see what he would have seen.'

'What he saw was very beautiful, not that that excuses him, but it makes it more understandable,' Beth said, then taking the camera she added, 'May I ask what you felt during a spanking?'

'I hated him,' Natasha snapped vehemently.

'But what did you feel about the actual spanking?'

'Well,' she thought for a moment, 'I don't suppose, deep down, that I really minded the spanking. Actually, I think it was probably quite a turn on. I just hated him, he was such a bullying creep.'

'But if it was someone else spanking you?' Beth persisted.

Natasha raised her eyes to the ceiling, carefully assessing the question again. 'I wouldn't mind, I think. It depends on who, though.'

Beth turned to Celeste with a triumphant smile. 'I told you she was one of us,' she said.

'One of us?' Natasha asked, raising a questioning eyebrow.

Celeste moved to the sofa to sit beside her. She took one of Natasha's hands in hers. 'One of us,' she confirmed. 'And as your place is so squalid, why don't you move in here?' She looked to Beth for approval. 'She could move into my room – and share my bed until we get another one for her.'

'No,' Beth countered, 'that is not an option. You seem to forget, my dear young lodger, that this is my flat, so I decide who moves in and who shares with who. So, Natasha can share my room... and my bed.' She smiled calculatingly. 'My bed is bigger, after all.'

Celeste made a moue of disapproval and cast a mean look in Beth's direction. 'Go on, be like that,' Beth said, 'and our new flatmate will learn all about house rules and house discipline sooner than you think.'

As she was speaking, Beth tilted up her nose and started to sniff the air. 'In fact, if what I can smell is our supper burning, she will start her education as an observer this very evening.'

Celeste shrieked and rushed to the kitchen, returning a moment later with a glum look on her face and a blackened casserole in her hand. 'That's the tuna pasta,' she grumbled.

'Then we'll go out for supper,' Beth announced. 'Celeste will pay, and she'll pay again when we come back.'

Two hours, two pizzas, and two bottles of wine later, the three girls returned to the flat carrying two suitcases of belongings from Natasha's flat. Over supper, Natasha had found out what she could about the other two. She was much cheered by Celeste's story, how the girl, her own age and with a similar education, had in the space of a day or two gone from no work and no future into a career with prospects. Could she, Natasha, follow a similar route? She was bored with modelling and was quite prepared to do it just part-time.

'I've had to use all my assets,' Celeste had said with a slightly inebriated giggle. 'Especially the one I'm sitting on!'

'I wouldn't mind, as long as I was putting it to good use,' Natasha replied, also feeling the effects of the drink.

'All in good time,' Beth said.

Back in the flat they made coffee and began to get ready for bed. Celeste wandered off unsteadily to run a bath while Beth and Natasha remained behind in the sitting room. Natasha took Beth by the hand and thanked her for letting her move in. 'I feel that my life is about to change,' she said. 'I will do anything to work with you, to learn from you.'

'You will,' Beth said succinctly, 'but I'll put you to the test first.'

They could hear Celeste leaving the bathroom and moving about in the hall, and Beth called her in. She appeared wearing her fluffy robe; otherwise she was naked. Beth made her lie over her lap on the sofa, and lifted the hem of the robe. 'Spank her,' she commanded Natasha.

'I – I,' Natasha stammered, her eyes wide.

'She ruined our supper,' Beth pointed out, 'so she

deserves to be spanked.'

'Oh no, I couldn't,' Natasha protested. She looked pleadingly at Beth. 'I am more accustomed to being spanked,' she added, by way of explanation.

Beth picked up one of Natasha's hands and laid it on Celeste's buttocks. 'Spank her,' she repeated.

Natasha slapped Celeste twice, feeble slaps, and then stopped. 'I can't do it,' she moaned. 'She's too lovely.'

Beth spanked Celeste hard. 'What would you like to do?' she asked Natasha. She spanked Celeste's bottom again. 'When you see this?' And she spanked it a third time.

'I would like... I would like to kiss her,' Natasha blurted.

Beth spanked Celeste again. 'Kiss her?' she asked, bringing her palm down crisply yet again.

'Yes, and make love to her,' Natasha explained shyly.

Beth continued spanking her younger friend. 'Then you shall when I've finished with her,' she said. 'She'll have a nice red bottom and you can kiss it better.' She delivered a ferocious flurry of blows on the reddened flesh while Celeste moaned and wriggled but made no serious attempt to get away.

After a few minutes, Natasha reached out and grasped Beth's arm. 'That's enough,' she said, falling to her knees between Celeste's legs. 'Oh, you poor thing,' she murmured, burying her face between Celeste's buttocks. 'Your poor bottom.' She licked the crimson buttocks and then sank lower, her mouth pressed against Celeste's sex, her tongue probing wetly.

Beth was content to watch and stroke Natasha's silky hair, while with the other hand she stroked Celeste's taut bottom, allowing one finger to probe within her tight anus. She enjoyed the spectacle of her new young and beautiful friend bringing the other to a noisy, writhing climax on her lap.

'All for one, and one for all,' Beth purred contentedly, and put paid to any talk about the sleeping arrangements. That night, all three girls slept in Beth's bed.

Chapter Twelve

Talking to oneself is the first sign of madness, Beth said to herself as she studied her reflection in the mirror, but it did not stop her conversation. She was not mad, she was happy. The job was going well, Natasha was a good and willing flatmate who actually paid the rent from her modelling income without being asked, and even Celeste coughed up on demand now that she was earning a salary and could not plead poverty. The sun was shining, the world looked beautiful, and her mind and body were fulfilled – oh, so fulfilled.

What could be better?

But the reflection wagged its finger at Beth. At times like this, the reflection said, things go wrong. It is the law of nature. When your head is in the air you don't see the banana skin at your feet.

Two hours later, Beth and Natasha had checked into a suite at an ultra-modern west end hotel. Across one end of the lobby as they arrived hung a huge sign: *Power to the Future*. Dozens of men and a few women were darting around studying notice boards on easels, proclaiming the times and the places of various lectures and symposia. Some made notes on clipboards, others gathered in groups making polite conversation whilst trying to decipher their companions' lapel badges.

'It's all go,' Natasha said as they were heading to the lift.

'There's electricity in the air,' Beth replied with a giggle.

Power to the Future was the biennial gathering of the huge utility companies from across Europe and North America, and Beth and Natasha were on a scouting mission. The companies represented at the conference were among the largest in the industrial sector, and an advertising contract with just one of them could keep a relatively small advertising company off the breadline for years.

'If we've got to go to that conference,' Beth had said two days before, 'we'll go in style.' She explained to Natasha how the only way to make good contacts and to seek new business was to be there and to mix with the delegates. That was why she had booked the suite and why she was taking Natasha. 'With your looks...' she said, allowing her thoughts to drift.

Now, in the suite, she grasped Natasha by the shoulders. 'Do well here, Tash, and I'll introduce you to Richard Cross. You never know, you might have a future *behind* the camera.'

Natasha leaned forward to kiss Beth on the cheek. 'I'll do anything you say. You're the boss.'

'And don't you forget it,' Beth said. 'I have ways of reminding you,' and she lightly slapped the girl's rump.

Two hours later Natasha had lost some of her enthusiasm, having sat through a lecture entitled Generation in the Twenty-First Century without understanding a word of it.

'Shoulders back, chest out, our work starts now,' Beth said, when they met at lunchtime. She led Natasha by the arm through the swing doors of the bar. It was crowded but the girls, smiling and shoving in equal measure, secured a small table near the bar. They ordered drinks, realising from the scrum that they were unlikely to be served more than once.

Before she had taken a sip of hers, Beth heard a voice. 'Is it Ms Forrester?' someone asked.

The girls looked up to find a tall man of about fifty standing over them. His hair was greying but his complexion shone with good health and good grooming. 'Peregrine Merchant, Eastern Light,' he introduced himself.

Beth held out a hand. 'I know, I haven't forgotten,' she said with a smile. 'This is Natasha Perry.' Merchant took Natasha's proffered hand in both of his, and his smile widened. 'Natasha, do you mind if I sit awhile.' He pulled up a chair without waiting for an answer.

They chatted for a moment until they noticed someone at the bar waving at Merchant. He got up, saying, 'Don't go away, I'll be right back.'

As soon as he was out of earshot, Beth turned to Natasha. 'Listen carefully, I must be quick. Eastern Light used to have a contract with us. When that contract ran out they signed up with another company. No time now to tell you why. Anyway, that contract is running out in a month. They are punting around; everyone knows it. Try to find out what he's thinking. He's the chairman.'

'What, me?' Natasha said in dismay. 'Where will you be?'

'I'll leave you to it. He likes you, I can tell. And he loves girls; he pinched my bottom once.'

Natasha felt nervous when Merchant returned. As he sat down, Beth stood up. 'I'll leave you in Natasha's company, if you don't mind, Peregrine,' she said. 'I've seen someone I must talk to over there.'

Merchant turned his chair slightly so his knees pressed against Natasha's. 'I don't mind at all,' he said over his shoulder. 'You needn't hurry back,' he added quietly, his face close to Natasha's.

By five o'clock Beth was feeling tired and dispirited. She had talked to so many people without results, listened to two debates about arcane subjects, and swallowed too many cups of coffee and tea. It had been a waste of time; her only hope was Natasha. When she found the other girl in the lobby, Natasha's expression and body language told her what she needed to know, or rather, what she didn't need to know.

Natasha shook her head. 'Nothing,' she said. 'I tried, I really tried. I think he fancies me but he's quite cagey.'

'What did you expect?' Beth said hotly. 'Him to give it to you on a plate?'

Natasha took Beth by the hand. 'Don't be angry. I'm just not very good at this sort of thing. I tried everything…'

'And you failed,' Beth retorted unkindly. 'So it's time for plan B. Meet me upstairs in an hour,' and she strode off.

She found Merchant where she thought he would be, in the bar. He seemed pleased to see her. 'What a charming young lady you employ, Beth,' he gushed. 'You must be coming up in the world to have an assistant at your beck and call. She speaks very highly of you.'

'And she speaks very highly of you, Peregrine,' Beth said, and then took him by the hand. 'Only you didn't talk about what she wanted to hear you talk about.'

He looked at her in mock horror. 'You mean, this?' he said, holding up his briefcase. He clutched it to his chest with his arms around it. 'You mean she wanted to see inside this with those great big, beautiful eyes.'

'Is that where it is?' Beth asked.

He laughed. 'My dear girl, that's for me to know and you to find out,' he said, and then became serious. 'I'm not a fool, you know, Beth. I knew what you two were up to.'

'I know you're not a fool, Peregrine. But your contract with the company I shall not name is coming to an end. You could give me a clue about the way you're thinking.'

He considered her words for a while. 'A clue,' he said eventually. 'Now let me see, what would that be worth? At least drinks and supper, I would say. On your expense account.'

'Seven o'clock,' Beth said. 'Upstairs, in suite one-five-two-four.'

At six forty-five in the bedroom of their suite, Beth said, 'Tash, whatever I say in the next few minutes, whatever I do, you go along with it.'

At six fifty Beth made sure the main door to the suite, the door to the corridor, was left slightly ajar.

At six fifty-five she called Natasha into the bedroom again, leaving that door slightly open too.

At six fifty-seven, she announced loudly and sternly, 'Natasha, you are a good-for-nothing, useless waste of space. Come here, I am going to teach you a lesson. Get over my lap,' and just then there was a light tap on the outside door, and Beth heard footsteps enter and then stop. At the same moment she smacked Natasha hard, across both buttocks. 'I'm going to teach you a lesson,' she repeated, and smacked the girl again, and again.

At six fifty-nine Natasha, crying, ran from the bedroom into the sitting room and bumped into Peregrine Merchant standing near the door, his face flushed, a lecherous grin on his lips. She shrieked in horror and sobbed even louder.

171

'Come back here – I haven't finished with you yet,' Beth shouted from the bedroom.

At exactly seven o'clock she entered the sitting room and smiled at Merchant. 'Hello, Peregrine, I didn't realise you were here,' she said. 'Just a minute, I'll be right with you.'

At one minute past seven Beth was talking to Natasha in a corner of the room. Her voice was a sibilant whisper capable of being overheard, and the only person other than Natasha within earshot was Merchant. Only certain words were audible. 'Deal with you later... very severely... tonight after dinner... my hairbrush... on your bare bottom.'

At two minutes past seven, Natasha left the suite with her head down to hide her tears.

At three minutes past seven, Beth took Merchant's arm. 'Drinks downstairs, I think, Peregrine. I've had enough of this place for a while.'

At four minutes past seven, Beth and Peregrine left the suite, closing the door behind them.

At a restaurant more frequented by tourists than gourmets, where the service was surly, the portions large but badly cooked, and the bill even larger, Beth and Peregrine Merchant eyed each other across the table. Both knew what the other wanted and each was determined not to crack first.

Merchant poured more wine into their glasses. 'You were very tough on Natasha, Beth,' he said casually. 'I couldn't help hearing. What had she done?'

'Not enough,' Beth replied briskly. She changed her tone and looked up at him from under her eyelashes. 'You could at least give me an idea of how many companies are in the running,' she said, completely changing the subject.

'Six,' he disclosed frankly. 'She's a very pretty girl; I'm surprised she puts up with it,' he commented, bringing the subject back to where he preferred it.

'She's a very naughty girl and she has to put up with it if she wants to work for me,' Beth said. 'Is Cross, Carstairs and Denton one of the six? Surely you can tell me that.'

'It could be,' Merchant said, nodding inscrutably and reaching for his glass. 'Are you really going to be... to be punishing her later?'

'I could be,' Beth teased, matching his inscrutability. 'Will you tell me if we're on the list?'

'I might do, if you do.'

'And I might do, if you do.'

'Yes, you are on the list,' Merchant conceded.

'Yes, I am going to spank her,' Beth told him.

'Is there any way I could assist, or at least be there?' Merchant asked.

'Is there any way I could assist our chances to get to the top of the list?' Beth replied.

'Possibly,' said Merchant.

'And possibly to you, too,' Beth said, and they smiled knowingly at each other. 'But the trouble with this arrangement,' Beth went on ruefully, 'is that I have to declare my hand before you do.'

Merchant took one of Beth's hands in his own and looked at it, lying on his palm. 'And a very pretty hand it is too. I hope it is a firm hand.'

Beth looked at him carefully. 'What exactly do you want, Perry?' she asked.

'Just to be there at the time.'

'Discreetly?'

'*Very* discreetly,' he confirmed.

'And what do I get in return?'

He squeezed her hand and then let it go. 'I can make no promises,' he said. 'Not yet, at least. But I can tell you this: I am looking much more favourably on Cross, Carstairs and Denton now that I know you are still there, working so diligently for your clients and with such a pretty, willing and naughty assistant.'

He raised his glass. 'To the future.'

Beth raised hers. 'To the future, together.'

'Mm, I like the sound of together,' he said. 'You've always been one of my favourites, Beth.'

She laughed. 'I gathered that. I've still got the bruise on my bottom where you pinched me.'

'Me, pinch you?' he said, in mock offence and innocence. 'Never, surely.'

When she called for the bill, he raised his glass again. 'To the *very* near future,' he said.

Beth looked at her watch. 'Indeed, about half an hour from now?' she said.

Twenty-five minutes later Beth was back in her suite, making sure to leave the main door unlocked. She found Natasha in the bedroom, lying on her stomach on the big bed, glumly staring at the television in the corner. She had changed into pyjamas and her hair was loose.

She seemed pleased to see Beth. 'Good dinner?' she asked, rolling over onto her back and stretching with her hands balled into fists.

'Not bad,' Beth replied, thinking that Natasha looked like a kitten when she stretched.

'Any progress?' Natasha asked, with a hopeful look.

'More than you achieved,' she said, then emptied her handbag noisily on the dressing table, listening out for the telltale sounds she expected. Sure enough, as she dropped her powder compact on the glass top with a clatter, she heard the slight squeak of the door and soft footfalls in the other room.

Natasha, apparently totally unaware of the extraneous noises, followed with her eyes as Beth walked around the room. 'I did do my best, you know,' she said earnestly.

Beth stood over her, as she lay on the bed. 'That may be, but it wasn't good enough, was it?'

Natasha hung her head. 'No, I'm sorry I let you down.'

Beth was unrelenting. 'So we have some unfinished business with my hairbrush.'

Natasha looked up in surprise. 'Oh, but I thought that was just a game to get the old goat going.'

'No, no, that was no game,' Beth assured her. 'I'm going to have a quick shower now, and when I come back you will be naked and waiting.'

As Beth showered rapidly, she wondered how Merchant was enjoying being the audience. Natasha naked and waiting timidly on the bed would be quite an appetiser for him – the overture before the grand opera.

When she reappeared in the bedroom wearing only the hotel's white bathrobe, Natasha was indeed naked, lying on the bed again on her stomach, with the hairbrush loosely held in her hands, tears of trepidation sparkling in the corners of her eyes.

'I don't mind being punished by you, Beth,' she said meekly. 'I am just sorry that I let you down.'

'You'll be even sorrier in a minute,' Beth replied, picking up a straight-backed chair and positioning it beside the bed, in full view of the glinting eye just visible behind the crack of the bedroom door.

She sat down and without a word Natasha placed herself across her lap. Beth opened the girl's legs, knowing that her sex was pointing directly at the door. Then she lightly drew the stiff bristles of the brush up over the moist labia and between the cheeks of her bottom, over the small tight ring of her anus, so that Natasha shivered. Then just as lightly she began to spank her with the bristles, until little pinpoints of red sprung up all over the yielding flesh.

She raised the hairbrush, turned it over in her hand, and then brought it down with a resounding smack on the farthest buttock. Almost immediately she did the same to the buttock nearest her. Then she sat back for a moment, watching the blood colour the punished globes a bright red.

Natasha said nothing, but grunted when the third blow fell, and again on the fourth.

By the sixth her bottom was a fiery crimson all over, except deep down in the valley where nestled her puckered opening. As she was swinging the brush back again, Beth noticed that Natasha's labia were open and moist, like a juicy fig ready for eating. By the eighth fierce stroke Natasha was in tears. She writhed around and sank to her knees between Beth's legs, burying her face in the folds of the bathrobe covering Beth's thighs.

'No more, please Beth.' As the muffled sobs came from her lap Beth could feel the girl's hot breath warming her through the towelling. 'I really did do my best. I even took a peak in his briefcase when he went to the loo.'

'You did what?!' Beth exclaimed, pushing Natasha away so that she fell to the floor with a shocked squeal.

'Well, answer her,' snapped Merchant, standing openly in the bedroom doorway. 'You did what?'

Both girls looked up at him in horror, as if frozen for a second. Natasha turned her face, stained with tears, to Beth. 'W-what's he doing here?' she snivelled, a note of despair and incomprehension in her voice.

'I'd say it's a good thing I am here,' he answered for Beth, 'otherwise I would not have found out just how underhand and deceitful and…' he hunted for the correct word, '…how unethical you two obviously are. Going through my briefcase, indeed! It's an utter disgrace!' Merchant looked at Beth. 'And I hold you responsible.'

'But…' Beth floundered, 'but I didn't do anything.'

'Maybe so, but this would-be thief, this industrial spy, she works for you. She does what you tell her and I therefore hold you responsible.'

When neither of the girls spoke up, he went on. 'Either I take this outrageous matter further, undoubtedly costing both of you your jobs,' he paused, staring at them each in turn, 'or I deal with you both myself, here and now.'

Still neither girl spoke. 'Your choice,' he barked.

Still silence. 'So it's up to me, is it?' he said, taking off his jacket. 'Right, first we must even things up.' He pointed to Beth. 'Robe off and bend over the end of the bed.' Then he looked at Natasha. 'She gave you eight strokes with the hairbrush, so you give her eight in return, and then it will be my turn.'

Natasha looked again at Beth, waiting for her to lead. Beth stood up and handed the hairbrush to her. 'This isn't fair,' she said, taking off her bathrobe as she spoke. She was naked underneath. She lay over the foot of the bed, her bottom exposed, and Natasha hesitantly stood beside her, the brush held limply in her hand.

'Get on with it,' Merchant demanded.

'Sorry Beth,' Natasha said, and she swung the brush

so that it slapped across the middle of Beth's buttocks.

'Harder,' Merchant insisted. 'She hit you harder than that.'

Natasha swung the brush a second time, and again it landed with a dull slap in the middle of Beth's bottom.

'No, you can do better than that,' Merchant said impatiently. He stood immediately behind Natasha, gripping her right hand, which held the brush, and pushing himself against her shapely form, her hot and punished bottom against his groin, the rough trouser material chafing her sore flesh.

'Like this,' he guided, pulling back both their arms as one, and propelled them forward and down with pace so that the brush swatted with a ferociously cruel impact on Beth's bottom. She squealed as if she had been branded and slumped on the bed.

They repeated the routine five more times without mercy, and Beth cried out with the pain of each stroke. Natasha was crying too, mortified that she was being forced to punish her friend so severely, and uncomfortable with the possessive closeness of his embrace and the telltale lump that pressed into her tortured bottom cheeks.

Merchant then took the hairbrush into his hand alone. 'Now it is my turn,' he said, slightly out of breath.

He made Natasha bend over the bed next to Beth so that their hips touched, two naked and inflamed bottoms next to each other, four red and purple blotched buttocks in a row.

'I am going to thrash you until my arm hurts,' he vowed. 'I will brook no argument or protest. And then you will do everything else I want or I shall beat you again.'

Beth rested her head on one arm, gazing into Natasha's eyes, just inches from her own. With her free hand she reached for Natasha's hand, its palm damp.

Merchant took his time. 'Two of everything,' he said. 'Double the time and double the number of strokes,' he added, swinging the brush down for the first time, 'on double the number of miscreants.'

He beat each vulnerable cheek at random and then systematically in order, never once letting up. Beth and Natasha gripped each other's hand fiercely, trying to stifle their sobs. Beth was pleased to see Natasha even try to smile through her tears, but her return smile turned to a grimace as the wooden back of the brush fell like a branding iron in a particularly sore spot.

Finally Merchant tired. They heard the brush drop to the carpet and his panting breath as he studied his handiwork for long seconds.

When he had recovered his composure, he ordered them to lie on the bed, head to toe. 'Guess what you are going to do now, while I undress,' he goaded. 'The last one to come will be beaten again.'

Beth slid her head forward as Natasha raised her upper leg. She nestled her face into the girl's groin, feeling Natasha doing the same to her, the same way at the same time. Beth gently kissed the younger girl's sex as her nose burrowed between Natasha's buttocks, the scalding flesh warming her forehead and cheeks. Lovingly she slid her tongue between Natasha's labia and deep into the already damp tunnel inside. At the same time she could feel Natasha's tongue tracing the path between her vagina and anus and back again before penetrating her own labia. Beth forgot Merchant, forgot the beating, and forgot the hotel room. All that mattered, all that she was aware of was the need to give and to receive sensual pleasure. She lapped her tongue up and down, and around and around

Natasha's clitoris, knowing if she brought Natasha to a climax, then she herself would climax with pleasure in response. She wanted it to last forever while, at the same time, she desperately wanted the release the climax would bring.

The heat of her bottom spread all over her body and she knew she was gasping and panting as she licked furiously at the younger girl. When the climaxes came, Beth had no idea whose was first. And it did not matter. Both girls convulsed, moaning deep in their throats and then threw their heads back and lay with their eyes closed, breathing heavily.

When Beth opened her eyes she saw Merchant standing at the foot of the bed. He was naked, his penis standing out from his body like a flagpole on the side of a building.

'I would call that a dead heat,' he decided. 'Now move over.'

He lay on his back between the girls and told them to follow his instructions. Natasha had to 'go south', to lie between his legs and to lick between the cheeks of his bottom and to take his balls into her mouth, while Beth had to 'go north', squatting over his head with her legs apart to suck his penis.

As she took the engorged head in her mouth she could feel his tongue tickling her already sensitive clitoris, his fingers running lightly over the ridges on her buttocks. After many minutes in which the only sound in the room was that of wet lapping and suckling, he mumbled, 'All change.' The girls obediently swapped places and the lapping and suckling resumed.

Then he ordered them to position themselves either side of him and to lick his penis in unison, from the hairy, broad base at his stomach, up the column to the glistening summit and back again. He placed a hand on each of their heads, the right hand on blonde hair, the left on black, to guide their movements and to synchronise their timing, the two tongues touching on their journey.

'Beth, you are the oldest,' he croaked, as he stiffened and his muscles tensed, 'so you can have the first mouthful,' so she obediently clamped her lips over his helmet and sucked avidly. Within seconds he spasmed and shot a jet of warm, sticky fluid deep into her throat. When her mouth was full she moved away and Natasha leant forward to swallow the next and lesser ejaculations, holding his penis in her mouth until it was flaccid again.

Ten minutes later he was dressed. 'I'd like to stay the night,' he said, 'but I need my sleep – and I don't think I'd get much here.' At the door he turned. 'You'll be hearing from me very soon.'

In bed the girls lay on their sides cuddling, Natasha's hot bottom resting in Beth's lap.

'Do you think he's forgiven us?' Natasha asked quietly.

'He jolly well ought to have done, after that,' Beth said. 'But I'm more worried about the contract; whether or not we're going to get it now.'

'It's hard work, your job,' Natasha said sleepily, nestling her bottom closer to Beth. 'But it has its compensations.'

Chapter Thirteen

At eight in the morning the telephone rang in the hotel suite. Beth shook her tousled hair and placed the receiver next to her ear on the pillow before uttering a muffled hello.

It was Richard. 'My office,' he said. 'One hour.'

'But it's Saturday,' Beth complained, still feeling drowsy.

'My office in one hour,' he repeated. 'And bring the other girl with you. What's her name? Natasha.' His voice was replaced by a heavy click and a dialling tone.

'What's up?' Natasha asked, sitting up and stretching.

Beth shook her head to try to understand what was happening. 'It can only be that bloody snake Merchant,' she said. 'He must have ratted on us and told Richard. Shit, he didn't waste any time.'

'After what we did for him?' Natasha yawned, then looked alarmed when Beth told her they'd been summoned. 'I don't want to meet Mr Cross like this,' she said.

'We have no choice,' Beth said, throwing Natasha's clothes onto the bed and heading for the bathroom. 'Our master has spoken.'

Sixty minutes later the pair threaded their way through the empty offices of Cross, Carstairs and Denton to the inner sanctum where they found Richard Cross sitting behind his desk, his face bleak with anger. He looked at his watch as they entered. He was wearing a sweater instead of his customary suit, and was unshaven.

'I do not enjoy spending my weekends getting early morning calls and chasing up recalcitrant members of staff,' he snapped at Beth. 'Explain yourself.'

'Explain what? Beth asked.

'You know full well what – what you two got up to yesterday.'

In a halting voice Beth explained as best as she could. She told Richard who Natasha was and what she wanted, how the girl had hoped to prove herself and win his approval with an unofficial, freelance job, how they had tried to elicit information from Peregrine Merchant, and how together they might have overstepped the mark of conventional behaviour.

Richard snorted in disbelief and turned to Natasha for the first time. 'Is that the way you try to impress me, by acting like some second-rate industrial snoop?'

'No,' she said. 'I'm sorry, Mr Cross, I was only trying to help… to help Beth.' She glanced sideways at the other girl for support.

He snorted again. 'Help? You realise you could get us struck off the register, thrown out of our professional association?'

When Beth tried to interpolate on behalf of Natasha, he peremptorily gestured to her that she should sit down on the couch behind her friend so that the two could no longer have eye contact, saying, 'I'll deal with you in a moment.' He kept Natasha standing in front of his desk.

'You realise you could be prosecuted,' he barked. 'You could be up in court.'

Natasha started to sob. 'But I didn't do much,' she pleaded. 'I didn't find anything.'

'I know just what you did,' Richard replied. 'Merchant told me on the telephone first thing this morning. He could still press charges.'

Natasha's dismay momentarily flashed into anger. 'Well then, he's a bastard,' she snapped, fleetingly forgetting the seriousness of her predicament. 'He already dealt with us himself. He had no right to tell you.'

Richard sat incredulous for long tense seconds, and Beth cringed behind Natasha. 'A bastard?' he eventually said, his tone one of disbelief. 'A potential very important client of ours and you call him a bastard?' He shook his head and rubbed his temples. 'And for your information, of course he should have told me. I should know everything that happens if it concerns the firm.'

'And did he tell you what he did to us in retribution?' Natasha ploughed on angrily.

'He did,' Richard said, a slight smile playing around his lips for the first time. 'He sounded quite impressed by the both of you.'

Natasha was indignant. 'He beat me – he beat the both of us.'

'How?' Richard asked.

'On our bottoms, our bare bottoms, with a hairbrush,' Natasha spluttered, her cheeks flushed. 'And then he rats on us.'

Richard laughed. 'Good; that'll teach you not to meddle in affairs that are none of your business.'

Natasha could hardly contain her fury. Beth could see her quivering with anger. 'Then,' Natasha said, clearly working hard to remain calm, 'then he made us suck him off. I whored for you and I don't even work for you.'

'Quite,' Richard said calmly. 'You don't work for me. And if you ever have any hope of doing so you'll have to learn, as Beth has, that everything is fair in love and war and business. How do you think I became managing director here?'

'I don't know, do I?' she said. 'By hard work?'

He smiled patronisingly. 'Yes, plenty of that, and also because I married the boss's daughter. My wife Helen is the Cross in Cross, Carstairs and Denton. I took her name when we married, to keep things simple. Is that whoring?'

Natasha shook her head.

Richard went on. 'I slept with her long before we were married. Is that whoring?'

'No,' Natasha said meekly.

'So let's get this straight,' Richard said. 'You did what you did voluntarily. Nobody made you do anything – right? You paid a penalty that was only fair – right?'

She nodded, and Richard changed tack. 'Do you still want to work here?' he asked.

'Yes.' Natasha nodded.

'Even after what you've been through?'

She nodded again, so he thought for a moment and then said, 'Well at least you show the right spirit. You have also shown enterprise, albeit misdirected, but you've a lot to learn. An awful lot. I'll tell you in a minute my conditions, but first I think we'll give you a practical demonstration.

'Won't we, Beth,' he said, snapping his head in the direction of the other girl.

'Yes, Richard,' Beth said respectfully, rising to her feet.

He also stood up. 'I hold you responsible for everything that went wrong last night, Beth. I hold you responsible for recruiting Natasha in the first place and for putting her in a position with which she could not cope. I hold you responsible for everything you two did to Merchant and everything he did to you in return. Natasha has every right to be angry with you—'

'Oh no,' Natasha interrupted, 'I'm not angry with Beth, it wasn't her fault—'

'So now you will pay the penalty and give Natasha a lesson at the same time,' Richard went on, ignoring Natasha's protestation. 'Bend over the desk.'

'But you can't beat her, please,' Natasha tried again. 'She has already—'

'Are you telling me what I can or cannot do?' he snapped. 'Do you want to make it worse for her?'

Natasha fell silent and Richard again told Beth to bend over the desk. He cleared away papers and an executive toy with silver balls, and Beth lowered her top half to the surface, gripping the sides with her hands.

He turned to Natasha. 'Lift up her skirt and take down her knickers.'

'Oh please,' she said, but he was unrelenting, so she did as she was told, whispering an apology to Beth as she raised the skirt and eased the girl's knickers down around her ankles.

'Right off,' Richard said. 'Legs apart.'

Natasha slid the knickers over Beth's feet and put her hand between her friend's thighs, pushing her legs apart. 'Look at those marks, Mr Cross,' she pleaded. 'You can't spank her again.'

'I can see she has been well punished,' Richard said, touching Beth's flesh. 'Peregrine Merchant is good at his job, I always knew that.' He reached into a desk drawer and produced a jar of lubricant. He handed it to Natasha. 'Put some of this on her.'

Natasha smoothed the oily paste onto the inflamed and purple buttocks. 'No,' Richard corrected, 'not there; on her anus, where it will do some good.'

Natasha looked at him in horror. 'You're not going to…'

186

Richard's eyes flashed. 'Are you trying to tell me again what I can and cannot do?'

Natasha shook her head. 'If you really are going to do it,' she said quietly, 'you should do it to me, not to her. I was the one who was naughty.'

Richard was unmoved. 'You'll get yours soon enough, I dare say. For the moment you can learn by watching. Now do what I told you.'

Natasha smoothed the paste over Beth's anus, which puckered at her touch and then loosened again to allow the greasy finger to slip inside. When the little ring was shining with grease, Richard turned Natasha around so she faced him and, pressing on her shoulders, forced her down to her knees. With no further instruction, Natasha undid his belt and unzipped his fly, sliding his trousers and pants down to his feet.

'Beth, watch,' Richard instructed, and still lying over the desk, Beth turned her head so that she was facing them. His erect penis was just inches from Natasha's face, and the younger girl took the swollen helmet into her mouth. Richard allowed her to suck him until his rod was stiff and full to bursting, and then pushed her away. 'Now the lubricant,' he said.

As neat as a geisha at a tea party, the dark-haired girl smoothed the lubricant the full length of the rigid column and then ran her hands up and down it in a continuous movement, gathering speed with every stroke. When it dawned on Richard what she was trying to do, he gripped Natasha by the hair and pulled her away from him. 'Oh, no you don't,' he said. 'This is for Beth.' With Natasha still sitting on her heels on the floor, he positioned himself between Beth's legs and held his penis with its head touching her anus. 'Now come and watch,' he ordered

187

Natasha. 'Come close.'

She crawled across the carpet to the couple. 'Closer,' Richard barked, and Natasha rested her cheek on Beth's buttock, feeling its heat, and stroked her friend's thigh with her hands, trying mutely to offer her support. Natasha's eyes were just inches from the rod that now began to seek entrance. She watched as it slid silently out of sight, deep into the most intimate part of her submissive friend.

The act was not lovemaking; it was brief and frantic, designed not for Beth's pleasure but only for Richard's. Beth gasped with every thrust, tears running down her face to form two small pools on the desktop. Richard seemed to be full of lust and anger. With each shunt Natasha sobbed in sympathy for her friend, and Richard rutted against Beth so aggressively that the desk moved a little, before arching his back and shuddering, and letting out a strangled groan.

Five minutes later the two girls with tearstained faces sat next to each other on the couch, Natasha's arm around Beth's shoulders. Richard was back behind his desk looking as he had done when first they entered the office, apparently untouched by the experience since.

'I won't keep you much longer,' he said. 'I hope lessons have been learned this morning,' he added sternly, searching their faces. They both nodded mutely, Beth shifting uncomfortably where she sat. She had hated the lesson, not because of what he did, but because of the uncaring way in which he did it.

He addressed her directly. 'Chester Hampton will be back in town in the coming week. We need that Internat contract. See if you can get back into my good books. Incidentally, it seems only fair to tell you now that Perry

Merchant was not just angry about your behaviour yesterday, he was impressed too; impressed by your ingenuity and your fortitude.'

He picked up a folder. 'You can go now,' he added.

'But…' Natasha began, but Beth spoke for her.

'What about Natasha?'

Richard cocked an eyebrow at the lovely dark-haired girl. 'You're still interested, after that?'

Natasha blushed again. 'Yes,' she admitted. 'Beth likes working for you and she admires you. I have not yet worked out why, but I'd like the chance to find out.'

Richard snorted. 'You're certainly a girl with spirit,' he mused. 'That's good. But it is untamed; you don't know the difference between being frank and being rude.'

'So?' Natasha replied cheekily.

Richard twiddled a pencil in his fingers. 'So before we go any farther you will have to prove yourself a willing worker, and to learn some discipline and manners.'

'From you, like Beth just did, you mean?'

'No, from my wife. Do you agree?'

Natasha looked surprised and glanced at Beth, who raised her eyebrows, a gesture that Natasha could not immediately interpret.

'And what would that entail?' she asked.

'You will spend two days in our home in the country, with my wife. She is very experienced. She will teach you and she will discipline you. If you are smart you will learn from her. If you are smart, you will also do what she says. Do you agree?'

Natasha shrugged. 'I suppose so, yes.'

'But that's not quite all,' Richard went on. 'You must also prove yourself to me. You will keep a journal of your stay, what happens and what you have learned, in detail.

I want to know everything. When you return to London you will present your report to me. You can write, I take it?'

Natasha ignored the last question, and asked one of her own. 'What will your wife be looking for?'

Richard shrugged. 'She won't teach you advertising, if that's what you mean. She's a bit out of touch. But she is a very good judge of character and a very firm teacher. She enjoys instilling a sense of self-discipline into young women, as Beth can confirm.'

Natasha glanced again at Beth and then said, 'Okay, it's a deal, but if I pass at the Mrs Cross school of self-discipline, do I get a job?'

'That depends upon your report; it better be good, it better be detailed, and it better be the truth. Remember, I will have already heard it from Helen.

'You can go now.'

As the two girls threaded their way back through the empty offices, Beth took Natasha by the arm. 'When I was young,' she said, 'we were going on a cycling holiday. Before we left we rubbed turpentine onto our bottoms.'

'What on earth for?' Natasha asked, pressing the button for the lift.

'To make them harder, so we didn't get saddle sore.'

Natasha giggled. 'Why are you telling me?'

'Oh nothing, it's not important,' Beth replied with a smile, hugging Natasha's arm closer to her bosom. 'I just thought you might want to buy some turpentine before visiting Helen Cross.'

Beth and Celeste sat leaning against the arms at either end of the sofa in their flat. Beth's feet were in Celeste's lap and the younger girl had her head leaning to one side, concentrating on painting Beth's toenails.

Celeste held up one small foot, to admire her handiwork. 'I have something to show you,' she said.

'And I have something to tell you,' Beth replied. 'You first.'

Celeste dropped the foot on the sofa and went off to find her handbag. She returned holding three photographs that she handed to Beth without a word. Beth looked at all three carefully and then looked up at Celeste.

'Great, aren't they?' Celeste beamed.

'They're pornographic,' Beth replied.

Celeste was indignant. 'They can't be pornographic, they're me.'

Beth laughed. 'I know they're of you,' she said patiently. 'I'd recognise that bottom anywhere. But they're still pornographic. Look.' She held them up as if Celeste had not seen them before. 'They're of you being caned in the nude by T.J. Kearns, who also happens to be in the nude and who has a great big hard on.'

'I know,' Celeste giggled. 'Isn't it exciting! He'll think twice before trying to get rid of me now.' She looked up to the ceiling in mock innocence. 'He might even promote me or increase my salary.'

'Have you shown them to him?' Beth asked, incredulity straining her voice.

'Just one of them. I told him to keep it as a souvenir.'

'That's blackmail.'

'No it's not. It's *cinéma-vérité*, or photo-*vérité* at least.'

Beth shook her head in disbelief. 'Who took them?'

Celeste looked triumphant. 'I did.'

'Oh sure,' Beth said. 'You took these from the side while you were bent over the desk having your bottom thrashed.'

'Yep,' Celeste said, and laughed. 'It was the remote control camera I tried to pocket when I was in Peter Parnell's darkroom. He lent it to me a week ago.'

'Not for nothing, I bet,' Beth said.

Celeste blushed. 'You're right. I had to pay with my bottom again.'

Beth shook her head in dismay. 'You're awful, Celeste.'

From a pocket Celeste produced the camera, smaller than a cigarette packet. 'It's great.' She held it out to Beth. 'I thought you might like to use it for your work, if you know what I mean.'

Beth pushed her arm away. 'No, I would not,' she insisted. 'You keep it. I don't want to touch the dirty thing.'

Celeste made a moue of protest and with a swirl of her skirt sat down again with a thump. 'So what did you want to tell me?' she asked, taking the photographs and putting them to one side.

'Now that Natasha is away in the country for a couple of days of strict training,' Beth started, and both girls gave an exaggerated shudder at the thought, 'I want to use this place for work tomorrow evening and I need your help.'

'Sounds like fun,' Celeste said, wriggling with pleasure, quite forgetting her annoyance about the camera. 'How can I help?'

Beth smiled at her. 'I want you to be Charlie again.'

'Yippee!' Celeste cheered. 'I'm quite getting to like Charlie.'

Beth explained about Chester Hampton, that he was a valuable potential client and she was doing her best to win his business. 'He likes games,' Beth said, reminding the younger girl about the night they spent in the hotel suite in central London. 'I thought we might use this place tomorrow for a charade.'

'With me as Charlie,' Celeste said.

'With you as Charlie in a mask,' Beth confirmed.

Celeste whooped with delight. 'A masked play,' she said eagerly. 'Let's plan it now.'

At eight the following evening, Chester Hampton stood outside the door of the flat checking the number. It was the right flat. He checked his watch. It was the right time. He recalled Beth's somewhat confusing instructions; it was Candy's flat but Candy would not be Candy, she would be Abigail, and she would be there with a 'friend'. The front door would be unlocked and he should enter and join in any activity or game he found going on.

So he turned the handle and went inside.

One end of the sitting room, the end where Chester Hampton sat, was dark, whereas the other end of the room was brightly lit. Abigail, dressed as a maid, wore a sexy black dress, the short skirt of which just reached the tops of her shapely thighs, black stockings and shoes and a tiny white apron. On her face was a cat mask and in her hand a feather duster.

'I must get this done,' she murmured, flicking the duster at the bookcase, 'Mr Hampton will be home soon.' She leant over to pick up a bit of fluff on the carpet, revealing tight black knickers stretched across a pair of saucy buttocks. 'He's so strict with me, I mustn't get in his bad books.'

She flitted around the room, bending and stretching, totally absorbed with the task in hand, oblivious to all else. When she was bending with her back to the door, a figure entered silently. The intruder was slimmer, with short fair hair and wearing a dark trouser suit and also a mask. The newcomer approached the maid silently from behind and smacked her proffered bottom. The maid squealed and turned to confront the intruder.

'Oh, Charlie,' the maid said when she saw who it was, 'what are you doing? Mr Hampton will be home soon. You shouldn't be here.'

'Well he's not here yet, so give me a kiss,' Charlie said, taking the maid into his arms.

The maid pushed him away angrily. 'You'll get me into trouble. Remember if Mr Hampton finds you, you're my brother. Now leave me alone and let me get on.'

She tried to continue the dusting but was pestered at every step by Charlie. As she reached to dust a picture he cupped and squeezed her breasts. When she bent down to the wastepaper basket he deftly pulled aside her knickers, revealing soft pink flesh and a shadowed cleft. As she moved he followed, insinuating a hand between her legs. Relenting, the maid stopped, threw her arms around his neck and kissed him deeply and passionately, but when he reached behind to grasp her bottom, pulling her even closer, Abigail pushed him away.

'Cool down,' she said. 'Better still, go away.'

But instead of leaving, Charlie lounged in an armchair, making himself at home.

'Well, occupy yourself with a book, or something,' the maid said. 'I've got to clean the bedroom.' As Charlie looked around, the maid added, 'But don't touch those in the bookcase with the glass doors. They're Mr Hampton's special books. He keeps a cane hidden behind them, to use on anyone who breaks his rules.'

As soon as he was alone, Charlie opened the bookcase

and began to read the titles of the books from the spines. When he found one he liked, he pulled it out and opened it. It was a large book with full-page illustrations. As Charlie turned the pages slowly, studying each picture with rapt attention, he shifted uneasily in the chair. After a moment or two, with the book open on his lap with a particular picture on display, he pushed one hand down the front of his trousers. The cloth emphasised rather than concealed the slow, rhythmic movement of the hand beneath. Charlie had his head back and he began to pant.

'What the hell do you think you're doing?' Chester Hampton demanded, entering into the spirit of proceedings.

Charlie leapt to his feet, and the book clattered to the floor. 'I-I'm sorry,' he stammered. 'I'm your maid's brother. I was just waiting for her.'

'I don't give a damn who you are,' Hampton said. 'You were reading one of my private books.' With his toe, he touched the volume lying open on the floor. 'The penalty for that is a severe caning.'

Hampton reached into the bookcase and found the cane, four feet of hard bamboo. 'Bend down,' he commanded.

Just then the maid hurried into the room. 'Please sir, don't beat him,' she begged. 'I didn't realise you were home. He's my brother.'

'That makes no difference to me,' Hampton retorted. 'I'm still going to thrash him.'

'But it's my fault,' the maid pleaded.

'Did you tell him to read my books?' Hampton asked. She shook her head.

'Did you tell him *not* to read my books?' She nodded.

Hampton swept the cane through the air. 'In that case

there's no reason to change my intention.'

The maid grasped the hand holding the cane. 'He's not really my brother, sir. He's my lover. If you are going to punish anyone it should be me.'

'It will be you after him,' Hampton snapped. 'The nerve of you, using my home as a clandestine meeting place. I can imagine what you get up to when I'm not here.' He turned to Charlie. 'Remove your trousers and underwear and bend down.'

Slowly Charlie took off his shoes, socks, trousers and underpants and bent down in front of Hampton, with his hands on his knees. With the end of the cane Hampton flipped up his shirttail and tapped Charlie's legs apart. He whistled quietly under his breath as he studied his victim.

'Take all your clothes off,' he said.

When Charlie stood in front of him, naked apart from her mask, her pubis shaved and her breasts firm and cherry tipped, Hampton said, 'You try to deceive me, on top of everything else. You will get double the number of strokes for that – double strength.'

When the maid cried, imploring him not to carry out the punishment, Hampton turned on her. 'Oh yes,' he said, 'for you too. This… this female is your lover, you say? It is unnatural. You are lesbians and you are deceivers. It is right that you are severely punished. I shall enjoy administering it but not until you each have had a turn.'

He ordered the maid to strip but to leave on her shoes, stockings and suspender belt. When she had done so, he made her sit down and take Charlie across her lap. 'Now you will spank your lover, as hard as she deserves,' he said, adding that the softer the spanking, the harder would be the caning that followed.

The maid needed no second bidding. She spanked until

her hand hurt and until Charlie's buttocks were bright red and she was squealing with pain. Then it was Charlie's turn, and she too spared no mercy, spanking even harder in return. The maid's bottom, deliciously framed by the suspender belt and stocking tops, quivered delightfully with every stroke. By the time Hampton stopped them, every visible inch of Abigail's flesh was a burning scarlet.

'Now for the real thing,' he said. 'Who's first?'

'I... I'll take a double dose if you'll spare my friend,' the maid said meekly.

Hampton laughed briefly. 'Very noble,' he said. 'And for such unselfish behaviour, I shall take you second.'

He made Charlie bend over the back of the sofa, and the maid to kneel the other side, holding her friend by the wrists. 'I am going to beat you for deceiving me, for disobeying my orders and for being a dirty little girl who plays with herself.' The maid watched with wide eyes as he positioned himself behind Charlie, cutting the cane in the air.

As each stroke landed with a meaty crack across Charlie's bottom, the maid could feel the girl's hands clench inside her own, and see the tears that sparkled in her tormented eyes. She sobbed continuously and hung her head, resigned to her fate.

'You may kiss her better and then change places,' Hampton finally announced, noticeably panting with the effort of caning Charlie.

With her friend still draped over the back of the sofa, Abigail went around to the other side and fell on her knees in front of the cruelly striped bottom. Tenderly she kissed the stripes, trying to draw out the pain with her soft lips.

After a moment or two, Charlie straightened up and walked a little stiffly around the sofa as the maid took the position she had vacated, the fabric of the sofa already warm under her belly.

'A double dose,' Hampton said. 'That seems only fair for a slightly plumper bottom.'

The maid said nothing, but clasped Charlie's hands firmly with her own. She gasped as the first stroke landed with force across the middle of both buttocks and she was crying freely by the time the last stroke cut across the top of her thighs. As Hampton dropped the cane, Charlie rushed around and started kissing the maid's bottom, placing a cool cheek on the burning flesh. Apparently oblivious to Hampton, she ran her tongue along the last weal until it met and lingered on the sweet lips peeking between Abigail's thighs.

Hampton, who had picked up the discarded book, looked up from the picture on the page that Charlie had been studying to the two girls in front of him. 'This gives me an idea,' he said.

He made the girls stand up and study the picture with him. It showed two naked girls making love. One was lying on the floor on her back, her legs apart. The other was kneeling over her, also with her legs apart. Each girl had her head buried between the other's thighs; each had a pink tongue against the other's red cleft.

'This is what you like, so this is what you shall have,' Hampton said.

He made Abigail lie on her back on the floor, with her legs apart and her knees raised. She wriggled as the tender flesh of her bottom touched the carpet. The maid still wore her mask, suspender belt and stockings. Charlie was naked apart from her mask. With her back to Hampton, she straddled the maid, her bottom in the air and her head lowered to the warm sex exposed and inviting in front of her. Instinctively and without further instruction, the girls placed lips to lips and started licking each other.

Hampton watched intently as he undressed. When he was totally naked, he too knelt by the maid's head, his penis just inches from her tongue as it disappeared inside her friend. Arching his body over Charlie, he slid his erection between Charlie's vagina and the maid's tongue and began to slowly pump so it was warmed and wetted by each. Then he withdrew, took the maid's hands and placed them on Charlie's pink and purple bottom. 'Open it for me,' he said.

The maid, licking her friend again, gently pulled Charlie's sore buttocks apart to allow Hampton free passage. As both girls increased the pace of their licking, issuing wet gurgles and gasps, Hampton thrust into Charlie's tight rear passage and started to pump slowly back and forth. This movement pushed Charlie's vagina harder against the maid's mouth, and Abigail thrust even deeper with her tongue as if trying to lick Hampton inside her friend.

The gasps turned to moans and the moans to cries as all three chased their climaxes together, and when their climaxes arrived, they came as a single explosion. With a satisfied sigh Hampton collapsed with his full weight on Charlie, and the two slumped onto Abigail.

When Hampton finally raised his head, he saw the maid's mask had slipped off, and he saw that the maid, the 'model' who'd been photographed being spanked and enjoyed fantasy games under the names of Candy and Abigail, was in fact the star of Cross, Carstairs and Denton – Beth Forrester herself.

Chapter Fourteen

'You look well. The country must have done you some good.' Richard Cross looked admiringly at Natasha. She did indeed look well, her pale skin tinted by the sun, and her cheeks gently flushed. The evening sun flooding through the window of his office turned her soft black hair into a lustrous dark gold.

'Thank you, I do feel rested,' she said.

'Rested? I'm not certain that's such a good thing. You didn't go to the country for some R and R.'

Richard Cross was, as usual, seated behind his desk. Beth lounged on the sofa with her feet up. It was Friday evening, after all, and the staff had finished work for the week. Natasha sat in an easy chair by the window, with a red folder on her lap.

'Is that your report?' Richard asked.

'Yes,' Natasha replied. 'I wrote it today when I got back. I used Beth's computer at home. I had to compile it in a hurry, so there are probably lots of mistakes.' She didn't add that Beth had helped her with the writing, lay out and presentation, even helping her print the report and put it neatly into a folder.

She stood up. 'I'll leave it with you,' she said, reaching to put the folder on his desk.

'Not so fast,' Richard said. 'We are all here. There is no hurry. I would like you to read it.'

Natasha, taken aback, resumed her seat, still clutching the folder. 'I'm not very good at reading aloud.'

'If you want a job here you'll find you have to speak in public,' Richard said, not too unkindly. 'You're among friends now, so it will be good practice for you. But before you start, perhaps you'll pour all three of us a drink.'

Natasha busied herself with bottles and glasses at the sideboard, trying not to look at the object lying on its surface until she had to move it out of the way. She pushed at it with tentative fingers, telling herself it was simply a piece of wood, not a cane. Beth, watching but not helping her friend, noticed the smile play around Richard's lips as he observed Natasha's hesitancy.

When all three had their drinks, Natasha resumed her seat and opened the folder. Richard nodded and she began to read aloud in a light, girlish voice.

'Tuesday, August 3.

'Arrived by taxi mid-afternoon. Big house, very beautiful. The central section dates back to sixteenth century. Enormous garden, complete with swimming pool.

'Mrs Cross very gracious, tells me to call her Helen. Tea together on the veranda followed by a walk around the grounds. Helen talks about purpose of visit. Says she was raised in a very moral home, turpitude was severely punished. (Looked up turpitude later in the library. It means baseness, depravity, vileness.) Helen says young women should learn obedience and self-discipline in an old-fashioned way, that infractions should be dealt with severely, a lesson she had learned at the hands of her father. Not certain I agree, not entirely certain what she meant, but kept silent.

'Helen says that she had heard from Richard that I had a tendency to be "light-fingered", and was an example of such turpitude. Her father would have been most severe.

Helen says the means never justifies the end. Must think about that. Helen says deceit is always destructive but most destructive when we deceive ourselves. She says the nuns who used to live in the house centuries before when it was a convent, used to flog themselves and each other to purify their spirits and that it was good for them. She calls it self-flagellation. I say I bet it was the monks who flogged the nuns, but Helen is not amused. She says I need purification.

'We sit under a huge oak tree in the garden and she asks me about myself. She is very easy to talk to. I tell her about modelling, how I am fed up with it and want a more demanding career. She asks me about my family and my childhood. I tell her about my time as a teenager in the hostel, how I was frequently being punished. She puts her arms around me and asks for the details. I sit on the grass with my head on her lap and she strokes my hair as I tell her exactly what happened to me and how unhappy I was.'

'Excuse me interrupting, Natasha,' Richard said, 'but this is news to me.' He turned to Beth. 'Did you know about her time in a home?'

Beth nodded, and Richard turned again to Natasha. 'Perhaps you will be good enough to tell me about it when you've finished your report. Now continue.'

'We make supper together in the big kitchen. It is lovely. New potatoes, cold meats and salad, followed by strawberries freshly picked from the garden with a sauce of crushed raspberries and cream. Perfect. Afterwards Helen shows me the library. So many books and documents. She finds some books that are more than a hundred years

old, maybe two hundred, about how life used to be in the convent. I think they will be boring, but they are not. In fact, they are quite naughty. There are pictures; Helen calls them plates, under sheets of tracing paper. Some of them show nuns being whipped. We giggle a lot but I feel quite sorry for them.

'Helen says it is time for bed as I have a hard day ahead of me tomorrow. She sends me upstairs for a bath. It is an enormous old-fashioned tub, and I feel as if I'm swimming, not bathing. When I'm up to my neck in water, Helen comes in and sits down on a bath stool. We talk again about my childhood and Helen says what I must have missed most, not having a proper mother, was bath time and bedtime. I am quite touched when she makes me wash well behind my ears and between my legs. When I stand up she wraps me in a large warm towel and helps me out of the bath. Helen is a strong woman. She is beautiful and the opposite of me, with a voluptuous figure.

'In the bedroom, a lovely light and airy room, she makes me lie naked on the bed while she powders me like a baby. I am not at all embarrassed in front of her; she does it all so naturally. First she powders my front, my armpits, my breasts, my stomach and lower parts. Then she makes me turn over and she powders my back. She runs her hands over and around my bottom for so long that I am almost hypnotised by it. She says she can understand why the man in the hostel spent so much time looking at my bottom because it is beautiful. As she talks, she rubs the powder over my bottom and between my legs. Her fingers touch me quite intimately but I am too dreamy to object. To be truthful, I do not want to object, I want it to go on. I hear her say that tomorrow the lessons in unquestioning obedience start, but I am listening not to

her voice but to her hands. She is a beautiful woman. I think I am a little bit in love with her.'

Richard snorted derisively, but Natasha ignored him and continued to read.

'Wednesday, August 4.

'Mrs Cross can be so cruel. I am awoken by her calls from the bathroom. I rush to her in my pyjamas and find her up to her neck in soapsuds. Then I say good morning and she replies, "Mrs Cross to you, girl. Now wash me". She stands up in the tub like Aphrodite rising from the sea. Her figure is as nice as I knew it would be. She makes me wash every inch of her, some areas, the areas between her legs, over and over again. I am soaked. Then I have to dry her. She sits on the bath stool and opens her legs for me so that I may dry in between. She says she always thought that a woman's sex looks like a ripe fruit, a fig maybe. I agree to be polite. "In that case", she says, "why don't you taste it?". I decline politely. Then she says that I am going to learn my first lesson, that an invitation from her is an order. She makes me remove my wet pyjama trousers and lie over her lap. She spanks my bare bottom hard. It stings like anything. As she is spanking me, she tells me that before the day is out I shall taste her forbidden fruit. In the meantime, my bottom will be severely chastised, that Richard Cross expects nothing less.'

At this point, a blushing Natasha stopped reading aloud and glanced at Richard, before reaching for her drink to conceal her confusion. Richard nodded. 'My wife was correct,' he said. 'How did you feel being spanked?'

'Like a teenager,' Natasha replied. 'Humiliated. Embarrassed.'

Richard nodded again. 'Details, girl. I told you I want all the details. Continue.'

Natasha replaced her glass on the windowsill and resumed reading.

'When the spanking is over, Mrs Cross tells me to take off my pyjama jacket so that I am naked and to wait for her. In the meantime I should clean the bathroom. She takes ages getting dressed so I have time to make the bathroom really clean. When she returns she is carrying a cane and an apron. She throws the apron to me and tells me to put it on. When I protest that I need my clothes, she says the apron is the only clothing I am permitted. I put it on. It covers my front, just, my breasts and my tummy, but from behind I am bare. I have already inspected myself in the bathroom mirror and I know that my bottom is red. Now I must walk around with it exposed.

'Together we go to the kitchen, Mrs Cross never letting go of the cane. I have to make breakfast for both of us. Luckily she wants nothing fried; I was worried that I might burn myself. But when I drop a cup, although it does not break, she lashes the cane across my sore bottom as I stoop to pick it up. I want to cry but I am determined not to give her that satisfaction. In fact the longer the morning goes on, and the more I am caned, the more it becomes a battle for me to show that I don't care. I see it as a battle of wills between me and the cane, a battle I am determined to win.'

Natasha looked up at Richard, her chin high and defiance in her eyes, as if implying it was him she was fighting. He said nothing but nodded encouragingly.

Her voice broke a little as she spoke to him. 'You said you wanted the facts, just the facts. I hope you don't mind that occasionally I put in my opinion.'

'As so long as it is valid,' he replied.

'I don't see the point of this. What is cleaning the house in the nude teaching me? Being thrashed like a convict... what has this to do with a career, with advertising? I clean virtually every room downstairs with Mrs Cross following my every footstep and lashing me whenever I miss a speck of dust. I hate it. If it were not for Beth, I would leave right now. I am not a fighter; I am a weeper. I break down in tears in the library and Mrs Cross softens for a moment. She rubs soothing oil on my buttocks that helps with the pain. When I catch a glimpse of myself in the hall mirror, my bottom looks like a plum, polished and ready for sale on a market stall, purple and glowing. I am so ashamed.

'She leaves me alone after that for a while. I have to scrub the stone passage leading from the backdoor to the scullery. I have been on my knees with a bucket and scrubbing brush for a good ten minutes when I feel a draft around my nether regions. I look over my shoulder to find the door open and a figure standing in the doorway, a man who is staring at me. He takes a filthy pipe out of his mouth and says, "In the country, that be what we calls an invitation". The brute was referring to my bottom. I stand up and slam the door; thankful my nakedness is fairly well covered from the front. But from that moment on, I feel always his eyes are upon me, even though he is not to be seen.

'At lunchtime, Mrs Cross says lesson one is over. She

allows me to get dressed. She gives me a white T-shirt and shorts and white tennis shoes, no underwear or socks. The T-shirt is very tight, as are the shorts, but after my near-nakedness of the morning they feel like a suit of armour. Mrs Cross says I must work in the garden in the afternoon under the supervision of the gardener, Ned Gudgeon. I fantasise about the gardener being young and good-looking but when I meet him I find he is the man who was looking at me in the morning, the man who saw me nearly naked. He is about fifty, filthy dirty and unshaven. He wears a slouch hat, old clothes and a leather apron. I could not tell you the colour of any one garment; they were all the same muddy brown.

'I like gardening normally but I don't enjoy the afternoon. Every chore seems to involve not only Gudgeon's supervision but also his assistance. When I rake the mown grass he stands behind me and holds my hands, holding the rake. He presses himself up against me and I can smell him. Even through the leather apron I can feel the pig is aroused. He makes me climb the apple trees to remove rotten fruit, and he stands beneath me. As I lift one leg or another to climb, I know that my shorts hide nothing. If he puts up a hand to help me it is always indecently placed. When I pick the raspberries, he reaches for my breasts, saying, "Here be a fine one, nice and ripe", and chuckling at his own pathetic joke. I feel like braining him with a spade. Perhaps I shall.

'When I finally go in, there are muddy paw prints on my shorts between my legs and on my buttocks, and on my T-shirt over my breasts. I feel as filthy as he looks. "I can see Gudgeon appreciated your assistance", Mrs Cross says.

'I cannot wait to strip off my clothes. When I am in the bath, Mrs Cross comes in again. She babies me. She makes

me stand up in the water while she washes me all over. I cannot help feeling aroused. Again I lie over her lap as she pats me dry and puts more oil on my poor bottom and between my legs. I can feel I am already wet there – not from bath water or oil – from my own juices. She leads me to her bed, puts me in it and then undresses in front of me. We lie together for a long time, with me nuzzling her breasts and her hand stroking my bottom. Gradually I feel her pushing my head down her body, to her belly and then to her sex. She opens her legs for me, and puts her thighs on my shoulders. "The forbidden fruit", she says. "Enjoy it. Eat it nice and slowly".

'Later we have a cold supper in bed together. For pudding there is a raspberry mousse. We eat it not from plates, but she licks it off my bottom; she says it has soothing qualities and will help the bruises. I lick it from that part of her anatomy that most resembles it in colour. I think I love Mrs Cross.'

'You can't make up your mind, can you?' Richard said.

Natasha shook her head. 'She's a very unusual woman.'

'She was unusually severe with me,' Beth replied ruefully, as Natasha took another sip of her drink and resumed reading.

'Thursday, August 5.

'The last full day, I return to London tomorrow morning. Mrs Cross says she is going out for the day, and I must spend my time with Gudgeon in the garden. I plead with her but she is adamant. At least I get clean clothes; I washed them last evening and they dried overnight. At ten o'clock she leads me out to the garden to find Gudgeon. He is weeding the onion patch. Yellow saliva, from his

*pipe, is running down his chin. To my horror, Mrs Cross
tells him to cut himself a willow switch because he "will
need it". He chuckles, takes out a knife and goes off.*

'As soon as Mrs Cross has gone, I hide among the
rhododendron bushes. I crouch down on all fours under a
low branch. For minutes on end I can hear the old fool
stumbling around looking for me, calling, "Come out,
Come out, wherever you are", as if it is some child's game.
Then just as I think he's forgotten about me and given up,
there is a loud swish and the willow switch lands with a
crack across my bottom. "Gotcher", the horrible old man
cries, laughing so much it looks as if the one remaining
tooth in his head will fall out.

'He tells me he is draining the swimming pool and that
I must clean it out. He has other tasks but he will come
back every thirty minutes or so to see how I am getting
on.

'It is lovely to be alone in the sunshine in the garden. I
wish the pool was full, but it is not. It still has about two
feet of water in it, the drain being plugged with leaves
and other debris. I get in and clean the sides as best I
can. When I look up I can see Gudgeon watching me. He
tells me I am going to have to get really wet to free the
drain and clean the rest. I wait for him to go, but he
doesn't. He just stands there, watching me and directing
with his stick.

'It takes me ages to free the drain and by the time I am
finished I am soaking wet. I notice with horror that my
white clothes are virtually transparent, and my nipples
are clearly visible through the cloth. I try to stand with
my back to him as I wipe up the debris, but I am sure
when I bend over he can see the shadowy valley of my
bottom. To my relief he tells me that he is going off to*

have his lunch. The sky has clouded over and I am quite cold but I wait five minutes before getting out of the pool. There is no sign of Gudgeon. I make a dash for the house but find the back door is locked and the windows are closed. There is no other choice but the tool shed.

'Inside it is beautifully warm and cosy and smells of dried earth. It holds the heat of the sun and I wish I had found it earlier. When the door opens, though, Gudgeon is standing there and I realise its disadvantage; there is nowhere for me to run. The disgusting pig says we can have lunch together; he has his bread and cheese for himself and that he will find me something to eat. I can guess what he means and tell him to get lost. He waves the stick in the air and tells me there is an alternative; we could go down to the local together and have lunch there. I would have to go as I am, in wet, skimpy clothes, but he was sure the men in the pub would not mind. Which is it to be? I tell him that I am not going anywhere and he pretends to be kind and thoughtful. I should give him my wet clothes otherwise I'll catch a cold. When I refuse, he cuts the air with the stick. What am I to do? I turn my back on him, pull up my T-shirt and push my shorts down over my hips. When I am naked I reach for an old sack to cover myself and then face him. His eyes are glued to my body and he seems amused. When I look down, I see the sack is crawling with lice. I scream and throw it away. Now I am naked in front of him, my last defence has gone.

'He sees my nakedness as an open invitation and begins to take off his leather apron. It strikes me I have two choices, bad and worse. Either I can do what he wants, bad, or I can refuse and then no doubt he will thrash me and presumably take me by force anyway, worse. He must

210

have read my decision in my eyes because he asks, as if he is asking if I want sugar in my tea, where I would like it. I don't need telling what "it" is. He says he would prefer my arse. I think he actually thinks he is being helpful and polite. That's one wish he is not going to get. Nor am I going to fuck him. I say nothing but give my answer by kneeling down in front of him, my knees pressing uncomfortably into bits of gravel on the floor. I start to fumble with his trousers, undoing the string tied around his waist and wrestling with old fly buttons.

'I finally get "it" free, probably the first time in months it has seen daylight. He is hung like a stallion. It is half erect and waves around in front of my nose like the trunk of an elephant smelling the air for water. I begin to massage it with my hands. He's not having that. He twists my hair painfully, forcing my head closer. I take the tip in my mouth. It soon becomes as hard as a rake under the attention of my tongue. After a minute or two of sucking, I hear him say, "Tits". I do not understand what he means so I ignore him. He speaks again. "Use yer boobies". I am glad to get my mouth and my hands off him. I mould my breasts around his shaft and continue to rock up and down. Then he presses my head down on it again, so not only is my jaw aching but my neck as well. It takes an age. The seed inside him must have dried up so that only the husks remain. A gardener without seed; that's an irony. I would have been amused if I wasn't the one doing the digging, so to speak. I wish Helen would come home. She would be horrified, finding a young girl naked and on her knees, with her mouth open and the gardener's cock rammed down her throat. She might have saved me, but Helen is out for the day; there is no last minute saviour. There is nothing for it but to go through with it to the end.

'Eventually my hard work begins to pay off; those doors inside him that have been closed for years begin to swing open. I can hear him panting and feel his cock getting even larger and harder. I can hardly breathe. As I feel his muscles tense, a sign that his ejaculation is on the way, I turn my head away and masturbate him furiously with my hands. He snarls in anger and roughly shoves my head back down again, holding me as he wants me, pushing himself deeper into my throat. I think I am going to suffocate. Just as I can take no more, he comes. The first spasm hits the back of my throat. He lets go of me so I whip my head to one side, swallowing and gasping for breath. His second ejaculation hits me in the eye and runs down my cheek. Some of it is in my hair. I have never been so humiliated in my life.

'As he gets dressed without so much as a thank you, I sit naked on the filthy floor, my tears mixing with his come on my cheeks.'

Natasha stopped reading. 'Detailed enough for you, Richard?' she asked indignantly.

'Yes,' he replied calmly. 'Very graphic. Well written, too. It is good to know that you were so charitable to a common labourer. What do you think, Beth?'

Beth looked at Natasha. 'You didn't say whether you enjoyed it.'

'In retrospect, I suppose I must have done. I was horny that evening. At the time it was the dirt I hated. He and the place were both so filthy. Let me go on.'

'Having got what he wanted, Gudgeon slinks off. With Mrs Cross away, he isn't going to hang around unnecessarily and at least I don't have to do any more work. Naked as

*a jaybird, I stand in the empty swimming pool and run
water from a hose over myself, washing away the touch
and the taste of him. I wash my clothes as well. With my
clothes wet and the sun again out and hot, I sunbathe in
the nude on the lawn outside the back door. It's lovely,
the most lovely two or three hours of the weekend. I lie on
my back in the sun, thinking of everything that has
happened, and then I fall asleep.'*

Richard Cross interjected again. 'I feel you may have
missed out something there, Natasha, before you fell
asleep.'

Natasha blushed. 'I don't think so,' she said defensively.

'Remember, I want all the details.'

'I've given them to you.'

'Have you? Are you sure?'

'Yes.'

'Then why are you blushing? Before you answer, don't
forget I warned you I would know everything.'

Natasha was indignant. 'I have told you everything. And
I am not blushing.'

Richard spoke quietly. 'You have not told me everything.
Don't lie to me.'

'I am not lying.'

Richard was persistent. 'Look me in the eye and tell me
the truth. Did you touch yourself while you were
sunbathing?'

Natasha shifted uneasily. 'I might have done. I don't
remember. It's not important.'

'I'll be the judge of what is important. Did you touch
yourself?'

'Yes.' Natasha bowed her head shamefully.

'Did you masturbate?'

'Yes… yes I did.'

'Did you come?'

Natasha was almost in tears. 'Yes… yes, I came. Are you happy now?'

'No, I am not happy,' Richard replied levelly. 'You lied to me and you left out important details. We'll deal with that later. Now continue.'

Snivelling a little and wiping her eyes with a small hand, Natasha took another sip of her drink before starting to read again.

'I awake with a start and a sore bottom. Helen has found me fast asleep on my stomach and has slapped me hard. She's not angry; she's smiling. She tells me I deserve a good spanking for not working hard but she'll let me off because it is my last evening. I get the impression she's quite fond of me. She won't let me get dressed, apart from putting on a robe until we get inside. She lights a fire in the sitting room and makes supper while I have a shower. After supper she makes me lie stark naked on the rug in front of the fire and tell her about the afternoon. I tell her about the incident in the tool shed. She shudders and giggles, but all the time as I am talking she is kissing my breasts and touching me, touching my sex. I can feel I am getting wet; she knows just what to do. When I have finished talking, she delves into her bag and produces a vibrator. "It is bigger and better than Ned Gudgeon", she says, "and is certainly cleaner".

'She runs it over my breasts and nipples, making them tingle, and then makes me turn over on my tummy. She pulls the cheeks of my bottom apart and puts the vibrator on my bottom hole. She reminds me that this is where Ned Gudgeon wanted to put his penis. It is a strange feeling,

the vibration on my anus, tantalising but at the same time slightly upsetting. Still on my tummy I lift my bottom into the air. She slides the thing into my vagina, which is more than ready. She plays it over my clitoris, which is absolute heaven, and pushes it in and out. She is such an expert I am putty in her hands. Within seconds, it seems, I am screaming for her to stop, I can take no more; my orgasm is so intense.

'I kiss her with gratitude, worming my tongue into her mouth. She tells me to do the same with her nether lips. As I am lapping at her beautiful clitoris, she reaches into her bag again and gets another dildo, this one with straps. She asks me if I have ever fancied being a man. I say that occasionally I have been curious, such as when I see Beth with no clothes on. She is so beautiful. "Well", Helen says, " you can practice on me". She helps me to strap on the dildo and we both play with it as if it was real. I stroke it with my hands as Helen takes it in her mouth. Then she lies on her back with her legs apart and pulls me down on top of her. I imagine I am Richard as I fuck her. I fuck her and fuck her, until she screams and orgasms. I wish I could come inside her.'

There was silence as Natasha stopped reading.

'Is that it?' Richard asked.

'That's all I had time to write today once I returned,' Natasha replied. 'There's not much more to tell. I left early this morning and came straight home. May I thank you, Richard, for an interesting few days.'

'It wasn't supposed to be *interesting*,' Richard said grimly. 'It was supposed to be educative. Show me your bottom.'

'Pardon?' Natasha could not hide her surprise.

'Show me your bottom.'

'Now?'

'No, tomorrow,' he sarcastically replied. 'Of course I mean now.'

Facing him, her chin up again in defiance, Natasha reached for her belt buckle. She undid it and unzipped her slacks. As she pushed them down, she turned with her back towards him. When they were around her knees she hooked her thumbs in her panties and tugged them down too, pushing her bottom towards Richard as she did so, and then using both hands to hold up the hem of her sweater.

'It looks unmarked to me,' Richard said after a long moment of contemplation. 'Perhaps you would be good enough to take a closer look, Beth.'

Beth got up from the sofa and knelt by her friend, to inspect the soft, rounded flesh. 'Hardly a mark,' she said quietly when she had resumed her seat.

'I'm disappointed in Helen,' Richard said pensively. 'I can see I am going to have to do the job for her. And there's also the question of Natasha's lie and the details she missed out.' Natasha was pulling up her trousers. 'No,' Richard said, 'take them completely off, and your knickers too. I haven't finished with you yet.'

With one hand on the arm of the sofa for support, Natasha humbly obeyed.

'Sit down next to Beth,' Richard ordered, 'and keep your legs open as we talk. I want you to tell me about your time in the remand home when you were young. Touch yourself between your legs as you are talking.'

Natasha leaned back, pushing her hips forward on the couch, her legs parted. 'It wasn't a remand home, it was a hostel,' she said, sliding one hand between her legs.

'Richard, do I really have to do this?'

'Yes.' He was adamant.

Natasha told again about her time as a teenager, about the warden of the home who liked to spank her, and eventually cane her for imaginary offences. As she spoke she began to pant and writhe on the sofa. Many times she lost track of what she was saying and had to go back and correct herself, constantly having to start incomplete sentences over again.

'Beth, Natasha seems to be having some difficulty,' Richard said, watching and listening intently with his chin on his steepled fingertips. 'Perhaps you would help her?' and without a word, Beth slid seductively to her knees in front of her friend. She pushed Natasha's hand out of the way and buried her head between the girl's thighs as fingers instinctively entwined in her blonde hair.

'Tell me again about the caning,' Richard went on, watching the beautifully conflicting look of bliss and shame on the dark girl's face, and the alluring sight of her breasts slowly rising and falling as she relaxed under the artful and audible ministrations of her friend.

As she tried to explain, her eyes closed dreamily and her cheeks rosy, she became more and more aroused until finally her last words crescendoed into a panted squeal, intermingling perfectly with Beth's wet lapping. Her head lolled back and she clamped her thighs against either side of Beth's head, giving herself over entirely to the orgasm that contorted her body.

A few minutes later, as Beth resumed her seat, Natasha fanned her flaming cheeks with her hands. 'Take your sweater off,' Richard instructed. 'You look hot.' Again she obeyed and dropped it onto her trousers, and now she was naked.

'Now perhaps you will fetch the cane on the sideboard,' Richard went on. 'I thought we might settle the score we owe you by re-enacting what you have just told us.' He turned to Beth. 'What do you say, my dear? It strikes me that she got off lightly with Helen.'

Beth nodded. 'Helen was much tougher with me,' she said, ignoring the sulky look Natasha gave her, and then watched appreciatively as the naked girl stood and walked sexily across the office, picked up the cane and presented it to Richard.

'Show me,' he said.

'Well, I would lie across the desk, like this,' she whispered, gracefully bending over the uncluttered desktop, resting on her forearms. 'I would have my legs parted,' she shuffled her feet apart, 'then the housekeeper would hold my wrists.'

Richard nodded to Beth. 'That's where you come in,' he instructed, and Beth moved to the desk and stood opposite her friend, then grasped the girl's wrists in each of her hands and pulled them to her until Natasha's breasts moulded softly to the gleaming surface.

'And then what?' Richard persisted.

'Then... then he would cane me, sir,' Natasha answered, her cheek against the wood of the desktop.

'Like this?' Richard said, slicing the cane through the air and across Natasha's trembling bottom. Natasha bucked and pulled at Beth's restraining grip, but without being able to break it. 'Yes, sir, just like that,' she gasped.

'Like this... and this... and this?' Each time the cane slashed down against Natasha and each time she acknowledged the stroke with a gasp of acceptance and of pain.

'How many would he give you?' Richard asked.

'Usually s-six, sir,' came the sobbed reply.

'Only six?' he mused. 'A mere two to go, then, so I'd better make these particularly memorable.'

Beth flinched watching the last two strokes. She knew how cruel and how accurate Richard could be; she knew without being able to see that they would fall on the plumpest part of her friend's bottom and that each would fall in exactly the same place.

Brave as she was, Natasha could not hold back her cries, and she was still sobbing quietly when Richard said, 'And then what would happen?'

'I-I would g-go to my room,' Natasha snivelled, 'and cry m-myself to sleep.'

'That seems a bit of an anti-climax, don't you think Beth?' Richard said indignantly.

Beth nodded. 'I don't think the warder had the courage to do what he really wanted to do,' she suggested.

'And that's the big difference between him and me,' Richard said.

'I think you should do to Natasha what you did to me the other day, Richard,' Beth said firmly, then let go of Natasha's wrists and searched in one of the desk's top drawers. Quickly locating what she wanted, she rounded the desk, unscrewed the lid of the jar, and began to spread the lubricant between Natasha's gloriously striped buttocks as Richard took off his trousers.

'Oh no,' Natasha muttered against her own upper arm, both of them still lying inert on the polished surface. 'Please, not my bottom. It's so sore.' But she made no attempt to stand up or to change her position.

'Oh yes,' said Richard, 'your lovely tight bottom it is to be.'

He positioned his gleaming helmet against the small, neat

219

ring of Natasha's anus and eased forward with his hips. Natasha moaned and gripped the far edge of the desk until her knuckles turned white, as her body responded to the inexorable penetration. Beth was forgotten as the two of them, slick with grease and eager for fulfilment, raced towards their separate but simultaneous climaxes.

Chapter Fifteen

'Are we going for fun, or the opposite?' Celeste's voice was full of nervous mischief as the three girls headed for the country in Beth's car. It was Saturday morning.

'We are going because we are summoned,' Beth said, 'and we'd better not be late.'

'If I know Richard and Helen there's bound to be a bit of the opposite involved,' Natasha piped up from the back seat.

They fell silent, contemplating what that might mean. Natasha was undoubtedly right. A summons to the Cross family country house was rare enough; a summons for all three of them was downright suspicious.

But their concerns were allayed somewhat as soon as the tyres of Beth's car drew to a reassuringly crunchy halt on the gravel outside the large house, just five minutes after the appointed time. Richard Cross was waiting for them on the doorstep, dressed in casual clothes and smiling broadly, the very picture of the perfect genial host.

'Let me record this for posterity,' he said, as the girls piled out of the car, and he held up a digital video camera as they primped and preened themselves for him in the bright sunlight. Beth was wearing a white linen skirt with a bright lemon shirt, her blonde hair tied with a lemon ribbon. Celeste was simply elegant in a red and white flowered summer dress, the skirt short and slightly flared so it swayed in a liquid fashion as she moved her hips. Natasha wore dark slacks as usual, and a lilac cotton pullover. She was so petit, making most men quiver with the desire to protect such a defenceless creature.

The Crosses were punctilious about formalities. Richard graciously put the girls at ease in the morning room, chatting lightly about the weather and the nearby sights, while Helen served coffee and croissants. 'I bet none of you had breakfast,' she said in a motherly way. 'Don't eat too much though,' she added. 'We thought you might like a swim before lunch.'

'I thought we were here for business,' Beth said, licking crumbs off her lips.

'You are, you are, but business with pleasure,' Helen told them. 'Business will come after lunch.'

'I have a special surprise for you all this afternoon,' Richard said, and Beth, who knew him best, found that slightly ominous, but she soon forgot her trepidation in the excitement of the other two.

'I didn't bring a swimsuit,' Natasha lamented.

'Oh, don't worry about that,' Richard said. 'House rules – we swim naked here.'

Having devoured the light snack, they went out through the open French windows and across the lawn to the pool. Natasha was the last to leave and as she set foot on the grass she looked about warily. Helen, glancing back and noticing her expression, returned to take her by the arm. 'Don't worry,' she said. 'It's Gudgeon's day off.'

Celeste was the first in the water. She flung her clothes and shoes beside a pile of towels and dived into the crystal water. Her head broke the surface as slick as a seal and she whooped with joy. 'Come on, you two,' she squealed excitedly.

Beth and Natasha needed no further encouragement, and in no time at all they were standing on the side of the pool, the sun hot on their naked backs. While they were still arguing about who was going in first, Helen pushed them from behind and they plunged into the water with simultaneous splashes. In retaliation, without consulting each other, they climbed out of the water and grabbed Helen as she was unhooking her bra and threw her in, still wearing her knickers and with her bra held on by one strap.

Richard stood in the shade of a chestnut tree, leaning against the trunk with the video camera to his eye, recording the idyllic scene before him. 'For the scrapbook,' he announced to no one in particular. 'And for insurance,' he added under his breath.

For an hour or more the four females played games in the sun. They threw shoes in the water and had to retrieve as many as possible without coming up for breath. They then raced two lengths of the pool and Celeste, who was comfortably in the lead on the second leg, realised it might be impolite to win, so slowed up to allow Helen to pass her. Then Richard made them do it again because he had missed the start. He wanted to shoot it from behind, especially when the four of them bent over to make racing dives. They had water fights in the pool, with Beth on Celeste's shoulders and Natasha on Helen's. Beth noticed that whenever there was any pairing up to be done, Helen chose Natasha, especially if it meant touching her in any way. Even though she lost the fights, Helen looked supremely happy with Natasha's naked thighs on her shoulders and the girl's sex pressed into the nape of her neck.

At lunchtime they lay, still naked, on the lawn, fanning their hair with their hands to allow it to dry. Helen trundled a trolley out, bearing a giant bowl of prawns in their shells, and dishes of mayonnaise, butter and thinly sliced brown bread.

'Perfect,' said Celeste, when she had finished eating, her lips greasy with mayonnaise and her eyes slightly glazed from some wine Richard provided. She lay back, and like a contented cat, was asleep almost instantly. Gradually the others dozed too, Natasha on her stomach with her head on Helen's warm thigh, and Beth with her head resting on Natasha's bottom. Richard lay back in his deckchair and allowed his eyes to feast on the beauties before him.

'Okay, you've had some fun – time now for work.'

Richard paced the floor of the sitting room as he spoke, glancing at the three girls in turn, sitting fully dressed, in armchairs.

'Let's see this as a sort of end of term report,' he went on. 'I'll start with you, Beth.'

She looked apprehensive but soon brightened as she listened to his words. He said she had been industrious and imaginative. She had won a new contract and hoped for two more. She had planted an ally, Celeste, in the bosom of a client company, and had taken another potential recruit, Natasha, under her wing. He said he admired initiative and enterprise and on those counts she had scored well.

He turned to Celeste. She had shown a drive and a purpose distinctly lacking when he first met her. At this Celeste blushed prettily but looked pleased. She seemed to have an aptitude for business, he said, and would be an asset to Cross, Carstairs and Denton if she joined the staff.

He glanced at his watch and then turned to Natasha.

She was young and had a lot to learn, but was undoubtedly keen and willing. He added that Helen had spoken very much in her favour. At this Beth stole a glance at the younger girl, but Natasha had her eyes demurely cast downwards.

When he had finished speaking and was glancing at his watch again, Beth spoke up. 'Thank you for your kind words, Richard,' she said. 'They allow me to raise something on behalf of all three of us, something we have discussed together. We would like to work for Cross, Carstairs and Denton but in a separate capacity, as an independent agency recruiting new clients. We think—'

'Beth,' Richard cut in, 'be quiet.'

All three girls sat upright, their attention again riveted on Richard.

'I hadn't finished,' he continued. 'I had mentioned your good points. Now let's deal with the bad. I have one word to say to all three of you: ethics.'

Beth was the speaker for the threesome. 'We don't know what you mean, Richard,' she said.

'Oh yes you do,' he snapped, 'but you think we are so foolish that we cannot see it. You think that by using feminine wiles and your bodies so wantonly you can manipulate men into giving you exactly what you want.'

'No we don't,' Beth said firmly. 'That's unfair.'

He cocked an eyebrow in disbelief. 'You mean you don't use your bodies?'

'Well…' Beth murmured.

'You know it's true,' he said, as in the background the doorbell rang. 'And I'm about to prove it to you. Helen, perhaps you would answer the door.'

The three girls and Richard remained silent, listening to muffled voices in the hall. Then the sitting room door swung open and Helen ushered in three men: T.J. Kearns, Chester Hampton, and Peregrine Merchant.

Beth felt her jaw drop and noticed that Celeste and Natasha had gone pale. Richard was an effusive host, seating the men and bidding Helen to make some tea. He thanked his guests for coming, saying that he was sure they would think it worthwhile, and asked them about their journey until Helen returned with a tray. Not once did the men acknowledge the girls and, Beth noticed, on the tea tray there were only five cups. There would be no tea for the girls.

When the pleasantries were over with, and everyone was settled, Richard addressed the newcomers. 'I gather you gentlemen have grievances about the working practices of Cross, Carstairs and Denton, for which I am indirectly responsible. I take my responsibilities seriously; hence I have invited you here today to try to iron out the problems and to try and make amends. First I think we should hear the charges against the girls and then we should try to concur on the consequences. Is that agreeable?'

The men nodded and Richard invited T.J. Kearns to start.

T.J. stood up and approached Celeste, staring straight at her. 'This girl was planted in my company as an agent of one of your staff,' he started. 'She took indelicate photographs at a sensitive moment and she has tried to blackmail me with them.'

Celeste was shocked. 'It was nothing like—!'

'Is it true – yes or no?' Richard demanded.

'Well, yes, but—'

'Yes,' said Richard, cutting her off and nodding to Peregrine Merchant.

Merchant remained seated but looked fixedly at Natasha.

'That girl may have an innocent look, but while working with a member of your staff she rifled my briefcase intending to steal private papers.'

Natasha hung her head and mumbled, 'It's true, but I have already paid—'

Again Richard cut in and indicated that Chester Hampton should speak. He got up from his chair and crossed the room to Beth. Placing his hand on her shoulder, he said, 'I accuse Beth Forrester of deception. She arranged a very private affair for me with a third party and then pretended to be someone she was not in an attempt to inveigle me into signing a contract with your company.'

Beth dropped her eyes, but said nothing.

Richard held the floor again. 'The case is proven, I think. Guilty, all three of them. Now we must consider the question of penalties.

'To win your trust, and perhaps your business,' he added with a slight smile, 'I suggest they should be severe. I am sure, gentlemen, that you have ideas of your own and perhaps you would like to consider them in the next hour or so.'

'But, don't we get a say in any of this?' Beth piped up.

'No,' Richard said shortly, 'unless of course you want to leave, but leave now and you'll be leaving my employment. Your careers, or your putative careers, in advertising will end instantly.'

He turned away as if sure of their answer and continued talking to the other men. 'While you are thinking, Helen has an idea to get the ball rolling. I don't suppose the girls will like it but they are hardly in a position to object. The offences for which they have been found guilty, and which they have not denied, are grounds for dismissal at the very least, and possibly for prosecution. If they are wise they will go with Helen now and do as they are told...'

The girls filed out silently behind Richard's wife. 'You may not realise it, but the central part of this house was once a convent,' Beth heard him telling the men. 'In the seventeenth century, the nuns were subjected to severe discipline...'

On a cue from Helen, Richard led the men into the library, directed them to armchairs and poured for them early evening aperitifs. The far end of the room was curtained off and from behind the curtains came the soft but distinctive sound of plainchant.

When the men were comfortable and each had a drink, the curtains drew back, pulled by an unseen hand and revealing what looked like a simple chapel, a wooden altar rail with a screen behind it. Kneeling in front of the rail with her back to the room was Helen Cross, wearing a black nun's habit. When she stood up her face was obscured by a white wimple. Three nuns, wearing grey habits and also wimples, filed in.

The first girl knelt down in front of the taller woman and kissed her hand. 'Bless me, for I have sinned,' she said in a clear voice. 'I have had carnal thoughts and I have practiced deception. I need to be scourged.'

'Genuflect,' said the 'mother superior', indicating the altar rail. The girl walked to it and knelt, with her back to those watching.

The second girl went through the same process of kissing hands. 'Bless me, for I have sinned. I have touched myself in an unseemly way and have practiced extortion. My flesh should be made to pay for my sins.' She took her place at the rail alongside the first girl.

Then it was the third girl's turn. 'Bless me, for I have

sinned,' she murmured. 'I have lusted after your body and I have contemplated theft. The lash will purify my soul.'

'Fetch the scourges and take your place at the rail,' the mother superior said to her. The girl disappeared momentarily and reappeared carrying a cane, a riding crop and a birch, before kneeling alongside the other two.

The mother superior approached the first girl and turned up her robes, revealing that she was naked underneath. 'Choose your instrument of purification and who should administer it,' she said.

'The cane please, administered by one of the guests.'

She turned up the second girl's robe, revealing another pink bottom. 'The riding whip please, from one of the guests,' the girl said.

The third girl was visibly shaking as her robe was turned up as well. 'The birch please, administered by a guest and by you,' she said quietly.

Helen Cross then picked up the cane and handed it to Chester Hampton. 'Scourge the flesh of my first novitiate so that her soul remains pure,' she directed.

Hampton took his place alongside Beth, as it was she who was the first of the novitiates, and swung the cane in the air as if trying to find a rhythm. Without a word, he started to cane the girl with hard, measured strokes. After five she cried out and slumped back on her heels, so Helen Cross stepped forward and helped her back into position with her hips supported by the altar rail, and the caning resumed. Twelve times he slashed the unprotected bottom, and each crack of impact was followed by a despairing wail and the sound of sobbing. Eventually Hampton dropped the cane on the floor and resumed his seat, panting slightly.

Helen Cross, the 'mother superior', handed the riding crop to T.J. Kearns. 'Perhaps you would deal with the flesh and the soul of my second wayward girl,' she offered.

Kearns took his place alongside Celeste with a grim, determined look on his face. 'Strip,' he demanded. The girl stood up, removed her wimple and pulled the robe over her head. Naked, she knelt down again, supporting her body on the rail. Without further ado, Kearns started to whip her mercilessly on her bottom and upper thighs. The beating lasted so long that Celeste, who had vowed to herself to remain silent at all costs, cried out for mercy. After five more strokes he was gasping for breath, and he too dropped the whip and returned to his seat.

The mother superior handed the birch to Peregrine Merchant. 'Punish the flesh of my third nun and drive out her sins.'

Eagerly, Merchant grasped the birch and strode quickly across the room to his quivering victim. He arranged her over the rail with her legs slightly open, and began to birch her bottom, making sure that the extremities of the birch twigs reached around buttock and thigh to the most intimate regions. Natasha yelped but made no attempt to move, so he continued until the floor around her was strewn with the brittle ends of birch broken by the force of his blows, and then handed it back to Helen Cross.

She threw off her wimple and robe, and the watching men caught their collective breath, for she was a magnificent sight, naked apart from a white satin corset, skimpy satin knickers, stockings, and high heels. Her eyes blazed like an Amazon contemplating war. She grasped the birch, still warm from Merchant's grip, and slashed two quick strokes across Natasha's already ridged and discoloured buttocks. 'You'll get no mercy from me, my child, despite what you may have thought,' she vowed, birching the girl for a third and fourth time. Natasha yelled again, but four more strokes fell before Helen was satisfied.

Then she ordered Beth and Natasha to disrobe like Celeste, and made all three girls remain as they were, naked and kneeling with their punished bottoms on full display for the delectation of the very appreciative guests.

Epilogue

A week after the meeting in the country house, Cross, Carstairs and Denton issued a press release. It said that following the acquisition of the Rybix contract, the company was pleased to announce it had signed long-term advertising deals with two giant corporations, Internat and Eastern Light. At the foot of the press release, there was another announcement that received little attention at the time. It was to the effect that Cross, Carstairs and Denton were creating a subsidiary company to be known as C.N.B. Holdings Ltd to handle the new contracts and to seek new clients for the parent organisation.

A year on, and the new company is doing well, so well that it may soon be floated on the stock exchange. There is no shortage of potential new clients; senior businessmen seem to enjoy going personally to the offices of C.N.B. Holdings Ltd. There is no shortage either of potential staff, even though they are all females aged between eighteen and thirty. The working hours are long and irregular and the duties are punishing, but the opportunities are limitless.

Helen Cross is the chairperson of C.N.B. Holdings, and Beth Forrester the managing director. Natasha Perry is the director of human resources, and as such she reports directly, and very frequently, to Helen Cross alone. Celeste Hampton, the wife of the reclusive Internat billionaire, is an executive director and enjoys attending all board meetings and personally interviewing all new members of staff.

C.N.B. Holdings was named after Celeste, Natasha and Beth, but the girls know a secret, a secret shared with an ever-expanding group of very select and intimate friends. It really stands for: Cane Naughty Bottoms. Look out for it in the city; it's there.

More exciting titles available from Chimera

* * *

All **Chimera** titles are available from your local bookshop or newsagent, or direct from our mail order department. Please send your order with your credit card details, a cheque or postal order (made payable to *Chimera Publishing Ltd*) to: **Chimera Publishing Ltd., Readers' Services, PO Box 152, Waterlooville, Hants, PO8 9FS**. Or call our **24 hour telephone/fax credit card hotline: +44 (0)23 92 783037** (Visa, Mastercard, Switch, JCB and Solo only).

To order, send: Title, author, ISBN number and price for each book ordered, your full name and address, cheque or postal order for the total amount, and include the following for postage and packing:

UK and BFPO: £1.00 for the first book, and 50p for each additional book to a maximum of £3.50.

Overseas and Eire: £2.00 for the first book, £1.00 for the second and 50p for each additional book.

*Titles £5.99. All others £4.99

For a copy of our free catalogue please write to:

Chimera Publishing Ltd
Readers' Services
PO Box 152
Waterlooville
Hants
PO8 9FS

or email us at:
sales@chimerabooks.co.uk

or purchase from our range of superb titles at:
www.chimerabooks.co.uk

Sales and Distribution in the USA and Canada

LPC Group
Client Distribution Services
193 Edwards Drive
Jackson
TN 38301
USA

Sales and Distribution in Australia

Dennis Jones & Associates Pty Ltd
19a Michellan Ct
Bayswater
Victoria
Australia 3153

* * *